# THE

# LIGHT

# OF

# HOME

# ATHENEUM

NEW YORK 1992

MAXWELL MACMILLAN CANADA
TORONTO

MAXWELL MACMILLAN INTERNATIONAL
NEW YORK   OXFORD   SINGAPORE   SYDNEY

# THE
# LIGHT
# OF
# HOME

## STORIES by
## R. C. BINSTOCK

Atheneum                              Maxwell Macmillan Canada, Inc.
Macmillan Publishing Company          1200 Eglinton Avenue East
866 Third Avenue                      Suite 200
New York, NY 10022                    Don Mills, Ontario M3C 3N1

Macmillan Publishing Company is part of the Maxwell Communication Group of
Companies.
          Library of Congress Cataloging-in-Publication Data
Binstock, R. C.
     The light of home : stories / by R. C. Binstock.
          p.      cm.
     ISBN 0-689-12156-3
     I. Title.
PS3532.I57L54    1992
813'.54—dc20          91-33840
                    CIP

"To Be At Home" and "The Passing of Time" were first published in the *New
England Review*.

10   9   8   7   6   5   4   3   2   1

Printed in the United States of America

*Designed by Cora Lee Drew*

For my JP

# THE

# LIGHT

# OF

# HOME

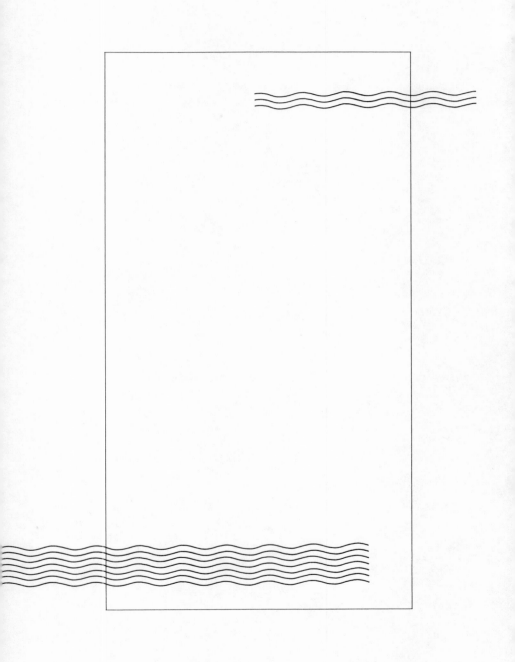

# · A
# Circular
# Shore

THERE'S a mood that takes Rachel—mournful, lost, disturbing. She's five. Waking from sleep, she stands at the top of the stairs, with her blanket; she calls to me in a different voice. I feel I don't know what to do. I come to the hall and say, "I'm here, honey," and she starts down. She doesn't want me to climb up to get her, or to meet her halfway; I wait for her. When she reaches the third step from the bottom I take her and carry her to wherever I was, and go on with whatever I was doing, as best I can with a little girl asleep in my arms.

When Esther went sailing away, leaving her husband and daughter here this island, I wanted to stand like Rachel, up in the lighthouse on the point, or at the peak of Bradford's Hill, and wave good-bye, and reach out as if to grasp the boat and lift it from the ocean and hold it to my heart, and feel my hand closing on empty air. I wanted to call out her name. Summer was over; the light was clear and lovely, but without warmth. I knew if I climbed to a high place I would see so much water, and Esther disappearing into it. I knew if I climbed high enough, if I pushed the horizon far enough, I could watch her cross the water and come to the city, and leave the boat at the dock, and vanish into the streets.

Now winter is at its greatest advance, like sheet ice, holding the island tightly. We stumble around town, in the darkness between our jobs and our dinners, huddling into our coat collars or hoods to escape the wind, sometimes with snow, sometimes with sleet, sometimes with salt spray or a faint salt scent, carried up to remind us of where we are.

When I pick Rachel up at Mrs. Underwood's house and we visit the post office to see if there is something from Esther, people smile if they can, if it isn't too cold or too wet to do anything but peer out with slitted eyes, and even then they wave. They like us, because Rachel is a pretty and happy child and I am soft-spoken and accommodating. Esther was very well thought of, and we were widely considered to be reliable, if new; though they disapprove of her for going, and feel sorry for Rachel and for me, they continue to believe that we are good people, and refuse to talk us down.

I know—because she tells me—that the postmistress doesn't understand how a man whose wife has abandoned him can be so pleased to get a letter or a card from her. She is puzzled because I won't (she has her sources) speak bitterly of Esther to the other men, but she gives us coffee and juice anyway, and pretends to drop airmail stickers on the floor—"oops!" she cries—so Rachel can scurry over and scoop them up and laugh.

Rachel plays easily with everyone: the other children, the neighbors, our occasional visitors and guests. I envy her her disposition. I don't understand how she came to be my child. Her curls amaze me; her smile, her laugh, her tight embraces are gifts from some unknown source, that I didn't expect or deserve. I had always wanted children, and when I met Esther it became fixed in my heart, but in the end I was overwhelmed, I felt almost embarrassed, as if I should have been the doctor instead of the father, handing the red and crying infant to some other happy man instead of holding it to my breast, wondering how I'd been allowed to go so far. Esther, without doubts, with a ready instinct for what her baby needed, would walk into Rachel's room to find me staring, mystified, love and confusion welling; she would draw her hand down my face, smoothing my brow, pressing her fingers to my lips.

Our house, which was too small when Esther was here, is cozy now, just right for the two of us. It's neither in town nor out, being a mile down the road to the south, toward the pond and what we all call the summer village, twenty minutes by foot and three minutes by car from Mrs. Underwood's and the post office and the grocery. We have a yard, with trees and a hammock for the summer, and two bedrooms upstairs, and a kitchen and back porch and living room downstairs, with a VCR for Rachel's videos (it belongs to Esther, but she left it for us) and two radios, and a desk for me that I hardly use.

The owners could get a better rent in July and August, but they charge us more in the off-season than most island landlords do. The total is less than it might be if they took advantage of the summer rates, but they don't feel right about forcing people from their homes every year, and they like having one constant tenant. "We wouldn't consider renting to people who don't have children," Linda once explained. "We prefer substance."

The house is old, and starting to fall apart—it keeps me busy making minor repairs, endlessly stopping by the hardware store— but we're attached to it. Even in the dark, in the wind that's always blowing, Rachel drops my hand and runs the last twenty yards and up the front walk when we arrive, to look through the window beside the door to see if Kittie is waiting for us in the hall, but also to feel welcomed home that much sooner. I like looking after the house and I've learned to do it well. It impresses Linda and Joe, it's a hobby, and it shows Rachel that I'm taking care; it teaches her that things need attention, that time passing brings changes to be reversed, forced back, as well as those that (like her) should be helped to blossom and grow.

As I make dinner, and my daughter sits at the kitchen table playing with toy trucks or stuffed animals, or drawing with her crayons, I miss my wife's warm body, the embraces from behind; I see her going about her business in the city. It isn't far, and it wouldn't be hard to arrange to join her, meeting her, for instance, at a favorite restaurant, in time for a good, long meal with lots of cheery conversation, and still to get Rachel to bed by nine. But I imagine her doing things that have no place for us, don't intend to include us, would startle and run if they saw us coming. If we surprised her, I don't know what we'd find.

If she came back to us, crossing the water again (crouched in the bow of a boat too small to make the trip except in the best of summer weather, peering through the darkness, chilled in every part of her, straining to hear the sound of the bells in our harbor) to knock on our door, she would find us just the same.

I imagine a coat tossed carelessly across her bed; I imagine her alone, in a taxi, thinking of me; I imagine the city and the island, tied together with a string, whirling around and around in a little boy's hand.

Every so often, as I'm frying the hot dogs or boiling the noodles, or trying to fix something or paying our bills as the chicken roasts in the oven, Rachel asks me when we'll be seeing Mommy, when we'll talk to her. It breaks my heart. These are the times when she should cry out, when she should be sad and lost, not waking from a sound sleep after we've played together and read a story and I've tucked her in and kissed her and she's sighed as she snuggles under, her dinosaur clutched in her arms and Kittie at the foot of the bed, cleaning herself, as I turn out the light. She should cry when she asks about her mother, who's gone away. (These are the times when I remember, Esther, that you brought me to this dark place. It's dark in the city too, but with neon, and store windows, and statues lit with floodlights, and thousands of people rushing.) She asks so casually, as if it didn't hurt, as if it were nothing.

Sometimes, when Esther still lived here, I would wake in the night with my chest full of pain, soaked in loneliness and despair. It didn't matter that I had a wife who shared my days, who lay within reach as I wept; that my daughter, whom I adored, was safe in the next room; that the rent was paid and the house neat as a pin. It was ancient; it was as it used to be, when I was desperate and sad; it was the whisper of a boy who tried, every time, to put the runt of the litter to the nipple, pushing the healthy kittens aside, and buried it in the front garden, beside the others, when it starved and died. I was dismayed, amazed to feel so strongly something I thought I no longer needed, but I waited—what else had I to do?— and after the first few times it became almost exciting, even pleasing: my heart beating, the ache in my stomach ebbing as I lay there, in the dark, feeling comfort return to fill up the hollow, finding myself in my own bedroom, after all, in my life, as if I had merely woken from a grotesque, familiar nightmare, as if I could abandon my grief.

Now I lie awake (with the lights out, and Rachel asleep, in the utter dark, missing the streetlight that shines through the shade in the window in the bedroom of my wife's house in the city) and think of Esther asking us to join her. Asking us to sail away, as she did. Asking us to leave this house. Would we ever see this island again?

Esther said: you can be on the island or off it; there is nowhere else. She is having adventures and we are here, together. She is feeling possibility, she is choosing to explore; she sees, from her high window, the roads that lead away forever; ours end at the shore.

I could turn on the light and put on my bathrobe, to stand by Rachel and stroke her hair; I could sit at the bright yellow table in the kitchen, reading the newspaper, with Kittie by my left hand and a cup of hot chocolate by my right; I could dress myself warmly and drive, in minutes, to the beach, to listen to the waves. All of this could crumble, could disappear in an instant, swept away. Would we see this island again?

Once, when Rachel was two, as Esther waited for me, I drove by myself, alone in the hills on a windy, rainy October day. In a moment, in a gust, the air around my car was filled with small yellow leaves, hundreds of them, circling me, carrying me, aloft forever as if by magic, as if autumn aspired to blizzards of its own. I was glad they couldn't share it with me. That it was all mine. The need to hold it, to save it, to bring it to Esther melted into a pool at my feet, and drained away; I was enchanted; my heart sang.

I keep Rachel, and the island keeps me, but I am no freer than she is; we both move, weightless, in very small circles, like tandem moons around a star.

# · To Be
# At Home

"THIS is awkward," she said, smiling, apparently to herself, in a way he recognized; he'd always thought she was laughing at him.

He said, "I didn't know whether you'd be coming, or when you'd be coming." She hadn't opened her bag while he was downstairs; it sat, plump and shiny, by the end of the sofa. The coffee mug he'd filled for her was empty. He flipped the pages of a book he'd picked up, looking at her all the while. "If I'd known, it wouldn't have changed my plans."

"Of course not," she said. She stood with her hands in the pockets of her gray sweater, near the window, stretching it down in front of her hips, over the black skirt that ended where the soft black boots began. She would not have worn these clothes when they were married. Though it seemed more or less appropriate for the occasion, Arthur found it strange, unsettling; she might almost have done it to distract him.

He'd tried to plan for this, in bits and pieces, on the plane. Unable to decide on anything, even to think about it for more than a few minutes at a time, he'd reminded himself that they had known each other well. There were many worries, all to be seen to in good time. "Do you dress like that now?" he asked, regretting it immediately, relieved when she smiled again and glanced down. The sweater looked imported and expensive; the black turtleneck under it reminded him of the movies they'd watched together. She was elegant, at least as appealing as she'd been in the brown and green, rough cotton, comfortable shoes days; he'd approved of her then, but this suited her better. He guessed that her dark hair, which seemed looser and less ordered, had been carefully cut and arranged. Her skin was clear and soft, her figure still graceful, slender but womanly, still striking. She had aged less than he, but had also become less a child, more like someone who could care for herself.

"No," she said. "It was for the friend I disappointed by coming here this weekend."

The room was large for a third-floor room in a house of this type, the ceiling slanted but high. His old bedroom, in the back, had gables; it was lower and snugger, like a poor painter's attic. Here there were two big windows looking out onto the road in front, though in the summer you could see almost nothing of it through the oak leaves. It was much nicer as his mother's study than it had ever been when his sister lived in it, but he had always liked it. In the big, old house, with so many rooms connected by an archway or a thin door, or sharing a bathroom, they had been constantly aware of each other's vague proximities, never sure who was occupying which space, or where one ended and another began. This room was the most self-contained. You could almost live in it, he thought, and throw the rest of the house away.

The floor, which had been mostly hidden through his adolescence, covered by games and toys, and stuffed animals, and clothes and books and magazines, was expansive, rich and gleaming around the small woven rug; the furniture was appropriately sized; everything seemed to fit together. His mother had given it careful attention. He thought the old desk was worth the eight hundred dollars she'd told him she paid for it, though he'd questioned it at the time. ("Pocket change compared to what your father spends on phono-

graph records and videotapes," she'd said.) It had many small draw-
ers and shelves, not the dark, regular pigeonholes his friends liked
so much but little display spaces and treasure chests, with polished
brass fittings, arranged pleasingly and neatly, not crowding each
other. He decided, as Laura put her hand on the window frame
and looked out, to come back, after the others had gone to sleep,
and see what was in them.

He had always approved of his mother's taste, and she'd frequently
asked his advice. The few reproductions and photographs on the
walls, which she'd repapered with something that resembled rough
linen, were the sort of simple, studied images he liked, and much
preferred to the grotesquery and bizarre humor treasured by his
father and occasionally forwarded to him through the mail.

"He drove me to the airport," said Laura.

"Who did?"

"My friend." She looked over her shoulder at him. "That's why
I'm dressed like this. Because I was with him."

"Laura, I know you have lovers," he said.

She seemed as startled as if he had filled her coffee mug with
lemonade, or beans.

"I accept your being here," he said. "In fact, I'm glad you're here,
because my father really likes you, and it means a great deal to him
that you decided to come. I was even looking forward to walking
down to the village with you. But I will not be required to be open-
minded and mature."

"I didn't intend to upset you," she said. She spoke softly and
carefully, her hands again in her pockets. "I wish you wouldn't
mistrust me so. I wanted you to understand that I wasn't making
some strange remark. At a time like this—"

"Not ever," he said.

They started together at a footstep in the hall, and he caught
himself looking at her as though they'd been found out. It was the
way they had always been, he knew, public and private, four separate

people wondering when they would meet. She returned the look, embarrassing him.

Sidney was almost smiling as he came in, and then he did smile, warmly, when he saw her. "Don't you look wonderful?" he exclaimed. His wrinkled white shirt was unbuttoned, his undershirt visible; he hadn't changed since the train station, which meant he hadn't changed since leaving his office that afternoon, the office he'd been sitting in for twenty-seven years. The lines on his cheeks showed he'd fallen asleep with his glasses on.

"Aren't you pretty?" he said. "I was napping. Did you arrive on time? Was Arthur waiting for you?" He walked toward Laura with his arms held out and stopped just short of her, reaching to take her left hand in his right while his other dropped awkwardly. "My son, the puzzler—to find a wife this pretty and then let her get away."

"Sid, I wish I could change it," she said.

"Don't wish that," he said. His smile went quickly. "It's a relief for her. And for me." He looked sideways at the floor, an old habit, familiar to his family. "No more treatments, no more decisions."

She kissed his cheek, stretching a little although she didn't need to—he wasn't a tall man—and holding tightly to his hand, which he tried to take back and then left with her, as though glad not to be responsible for it.

"This makes me think of so much," she said, gesturing around the room with her free hand.

Sidney shook his head. "Such a god-damned shame," he said. "She hardly got to enjoy it. She just recently finished it, you know. I loved our little ritual, where she invited me up here and asked for my opinion so she could ignore it and do what she really wanted."

"Art told me," said Laura, "that you weren't very happy about her care." Arthur was slightly shocked; they hadn't discussed it since meeting at the airport gate, nor could he remember mentioning it on the phone. Someone else had told her. She had once gotten nearly everything from him; now she gave him credit for what he hadn't done.

"It was so strange," said his father. "I was so discouraged. I should have been ready for it. You think it means something, to be an insider, to know what's really going on."

Sitting on the sofa—it opened into a surprisingly comfortable bed, in which Laura and Art had once slept, when it was new—Sidney looked at each of them, in turn, as Laura sat beside him, hands motionless in her lap. He took out a cigarette and she reached to the end table, to get the ebony lighter for him. "I can't tell you how many times I was in the hospital," he said, "in the emergency room or the wards, watching some miserable resident trying to cope with some hopeless case and thinking, 'That could be me. That could be my wife, that could be my children.' I knew I needed to prepare. I decided I would be strong and clear-minded," he told them, touching his temple, leaning slightly, "that I would be able to make the decisions I had to make. It was like those jokes—do I mean riddles?—where the surgeon says, 'I can't operate! That's my son!'" He sighed. "Such foolishness," he said. "Who better?" He looked very manly, lighting the cigarette and inhaling, all thick black hair on his forearms, next to his rolled-up cuffs, and wiry gray hair on his head.

"But: when it came to the fact I was useless," he said. "Worse than useless. Incapable. Because all I could think of was how jealous I was of my patients—they had me, but I didn't have anybody— and of the other patients in the hospital, all with their doctors, and how angry I was that it was so. There was no one to tell me what to do." A light flashed through the window as a passing car reflected the afternoon sun, and Sidney turned toward it. "No one would help me," he said. Taking the ashtray from Laura—she had listened patiently—he saw his son and appeared, suddenly, to focus. "I'm sorry, Arthur," he said, "I realize this isn't a psychiatrist's office."

"It's okay, Dad," Art answered. "You've had a difficult time."

Mortified, stupidly inarticulate, he looked at Laura, wanting her to draw his father out, to keep him talking. She watched steadily, hands in her pockets; he wished her away, then wished her back again.

"Nonetheless, you're entitled to experience your own grief without having to be an audience to mine." Sidney stood and took his glasses out of his pocket. "I came to tell you that Lindy and Grace are getting in at seven-thirty and nine, respectively—I thought we could all go out, and wait between their flights—and that the Zulalians are bringing dinner over in about half an hour," he said, fitting the temples over his ears, carefully, as though assembling something. "They promised they would just bring the food and leave us alone, but if you'd like to have them stay a while, feel free to invite them. They're very nice." An awful, jagged edge passed through Arthur as he gathered, with pitiless certainty, that he could not ask Laura to avoid the Zulalians with him and go to the White Tower for dinner. There were so many reasons why he couldn't that he staggered, briefly, under the depth and completeness of it. As Laura put her arms around his father and laid her head on his chest, as Sidney held her gingerly, Art saw an elaborate structure, multicolored and patterned, fall in on itself, rearranged; he pushed them in his mind to the corners of the room; he saw the skyline from the balcony of his apartment, shining in the sunlight, empty and still, parting the wind. He remembered the picture taken on their honeymoon, in Nova Scotia, as he stood in front of the restaurant—"FRESH FISH" and "EAT"—where they'd dined every night, and she stood behind him, hands on his shoulders, peering out around his side, as if she knew the future. It was like an unexpected snowstorm, or what his mother had told him about the voices on the radio, and her parents' faces, in 1939; the world had changed overnight.

# · About
# Every Person
# There Is
# Something
# To Love

IT isn't easy being Martha's granddaughter. Debbie knows other
kids who have it worse than she does: divorced parents, short money,
illnesses, drugs. But every day she comes home from school wishing
Martha wouldn't be there; every day she hopes her mother will see
how tired she's getting, how close she is to losing her smile and her
respectful ways.

It would be easier, she thinks, if I had a sister or brother. It would
be easier if Grandma weren't so big and so strong. I hate it when
she fights me. When she tells me what I do wrong. I hate the way
she makes me call her Martha. I used to call her Grandma when I
was six; what's wrong with it now? She used to be pretty and she
used to make jokes, she used to ask about *me* and how *I* was, now
she just sits there and shakes, or complains, or talks as if she's the
only one anything ever happened to. They rebuilt the whole downstairs for her—I loved that porch, it was my favorite place, now
you can't even tell it was there—and she couldn't say thank you if
she wanted to. She wouldn't know how.

Debbie's mother, a tired gray-haired woman, slimmer than Martha but not as slim as Debbie, often sits at the table and sighs after
they've put Martha to bed. After Debbie has put Martha to bed. She

makes tea, and offers it to Debbie, and sometimes takes a cup to Debbie's father in the study. All of this happens in a silence that would have been unthinkable in Debbie's house just a year or two ago. Debbie can hear the clock in the hall; she might as well be old herself. She wants to know whether her mother sighs because it's hard to hear her own mother spoken to as a child, or because she regrets making Debbie do what she can't bring herself to do, or because she's dissatisfied with Debbie, or because the presence of the three of them in one house makes it impossible not to think about the future, and the passing of time. I will be older soon, thinks Debbie; I will be a mother, and my mother will be a grandmother, and Martha will be dead. I will have my own house. Mother may live with me.

"You're pretty," says Zip, the boy with the black T-shirts from down the street. He has just come running up to her.

"It's nice of you to say so," she tells him.

"Will you ever baby-sit with us anymore?" he asks.

"I don't know," she says. "Probably not."

Zip cranes his neck and pushes his face toward her, bearing a strange expression. "You're really pretty," he says, turning his head sideways.

"Let's go on a date," she says.

He laughs. "Get real!" he says, and runs away.

She knows very well why Martha is living with them. Her parents don't make changes without explaining them to her, and asking her agreement; if they do leave her out they apologize. When they got the diagnosis her father made her sit down with him and told her about it, and went over the options with her, and the costs, and explained how confused her mother felt about the issue, how difficult it was for her to make a decision. "It's very painful for her, honey," he said. He seemed to be hurting too. "You must realize there's no schedule for this. No one knows how long the stages will last."

He turned over the yellow pad on which he'd written figures: so much per month for the nursing home, so much for Medex, so much for visits by the nurse, so much coming from Grandpa's pension and Social Security. "I think the hardest thing for your mother is the thought that if we placed Martha in an institutional setting she might feel she was being discarded. Thrown away." When her father is upset he speaks formally, using phrases like "institutional setting." "All she cares about is her family," he went on. "Len is gone and Nora is in London; all she wants is to be near her family."

"I understand," she told him.

He looked away from her. "It will require a lot from all of us," he said, as if she didn't.

In the mornings, when Debbie wakes her, Martha is bewildered and often a little frightened, but easily soothed with kind and cheery words. One particular morning Debbie can't comfort her; her eyes move around the room restlessly, endlessly; she clutches the covers; every time Debbie tries to speak she says, "Sh! Sh!"

Finally she looks at Debbie. "They're coming for the Jews," she whispers. Debbie wants to deny it, but Martha's great conviction deters her. "They're coming for the Jews," she whispers again.

"There's no one coming," says Debbie.

"Hush!" Martha tells her, "pay attention."

"There's no one here, Martha," says Debbie. "I'll get Mother for you."

Martha grips her: "Don't leave me."

"Don't worry, Grandma," says Debbie, disengaging. "Please don't worry. I'll get Mom."

In the late afternoon, before dinner, Martha is animated, filled with confidence and severity, issuing commands. It's her most articulate time, her most composed time; Debbie can have a real conversation with her then but rarely chooses to, because she thinks she knows everything. She says to Debbie, "Invite that boy here again. I like him." She tells her, "You mother wants you to snap the beans, she put them on the counter there, but I think we've had far too many beans this month, don't you?" She asks, "What's that schoolbook?" and Debbie must show it to her, and be criticized for studying the wrong subjects, or for not reading the book quickly enough, or just for being young.

She never gets to talk about it; her friends don't often come to the house, and they aren't familiar with her situation. Her mother knows, and her father, and Cecil, who takes Martha out on weekends; and she knows. They exchange looks, like plotters, like thieves. They are four silent corners of a star.

Sometimes Martha lets Debbie braid her hair. She is always surprised by how much she enjoys this. Her parents are pleased and relieved as they watch. It seems to calm Martha too; it seems to make her lenient, even forgiving, and to cast them as friends, as if the motion of Debbie's hands makes her into another person, a woman she has always known but has never managed to satisfy.

I'm being cheated, Debbie thinks one evening, walking back from her friend's house in the dark, holding her homework in front of her. I've lost something that used to belong to me. Suddenly I'm not the child of the house; suddenly I have to be grown up.

I was getting there on my own, she thinks. It's not as if I wasn't trying. They didn't have to look after me. I was doing fine, but *now I have to do even better. There's no place for the baby anymore.* She's amazed to feel the warm tears dripping down her face, to hear herself sob so loudly, but she keeps walking, hoping she won't meet anyone, feeling for the tissue in her pocket, nearly blind.

"You're wonderful with her, Debbie," says her mother.

"I'm not," says Debbie. "I couldn't be if I tried."

Every day she looks for signs that her grandmother is weakening, is fading away. She fears it more than anything in the world. Every breakfast, every bowel movement, every buttoned nightgown is a torture and a victory; each week she looks forward to spending some portion of the week's end alone with her parents, alone in her house, while Cecil takes Martha on her outing, and from the time they leave until the time they come back she can't be at rest. "Be careful, Cecil," she says to him as he closes the passenger door and straightens up, keys in hand.

"I will, sweetheart," he answers, smiling. She is grateful to him, in that he seems to understand.

# · Birdland

I don't know what made me call Sallie. Curiosity, almost certainly, and probably boredom and loneliness as well; I was in a town I didn't know, with time on my hands. I must have believed it would please my wife, which I wanted to do, though I mistrusted her enthusiasm for bringing together people who shared only her acquaintance, as if that were enough to guarantee a good time for all. Mostly, I think, I was eager to touch the life I'd so recently joined myself to, this woman I still hardly knew what to do with and understood so incompletely.

Sallie hesitated at first, as I'd expected; Nina had told me she'd be slow to warm. "I'm not available until tomorrow afternoon," she said, after asking a few questions, "but if you're free then and want to come over, it would be interesting to meet you."

"That would be fine," I said. "Is two o'clock a good time?"

"Yes," she said. Her voice was high and a little tired. "You're sure it's convenient for you as well?" I explained that the man I needed to see had gone away, to return on Monday, and that I had nothing to do until then. She was quiet for a moment, then gave me brief, precise instructions for getting to her house—she'd lived in the city all her life, she told me, and even knew the motel I was staying at—and was pleased to hear I had a map spread in front of me as she spoke. "That's so practical," she said. She laughed. "It's hard to imagine my Nina with such a practical person."

"I'm not entirely practical," I said, "and she's probably more so than when you knew her."

"I don't doubt it," said Sallie. "Look, I hope you won't expect very much. I don't know how easy it will be for me to entertain you."

I was touched by her directness, and puzzled by the suggestion of pain—she hadn't spoken with Nina in over five years—and also slightly annoyed. "No, I won't expect anything in particular," I said. "It's just that Nina was very eager for me to meet you." In fact, there were others I could have called; it was I who had chosen Sallie from the list. "She was very disappointed that she couldn't come with me, to introduce me and show me around."

"I imagine so," she said. "Well, be here at two. I can promise you lemonade."

After I hung up I looked around the room, trying to decide what I had gathered, if anything, from Sallie's voice and words. It was a typical motel room and it reminded me of the ones I'd sometimes stayed in, traveling around the country as a much younger man. In those days I bought magazines with pictures of naked women, and took them to my room, and touched myself as I looked at them. Alone and uninterruptible, far from my family and my confident friends, I pretended the women on the shiny pages were local girls to be picked up for the night, to be pleased and then forgotten. I always made it last as long as I could physically stand, as long as it quickened my heart, because once it was over there was nothing to do but loathe myself and go to sleep.

Sallie's reaction, I knew, meant nothing under the circumstances; I had no way of telling how upsetting or ridiculous or exciting it might have been for her to get my call. I wondered if I'd acted too soon, or misjudged my own inclinations, but now it was done, and meeting Sallie would surely be better than doing nothing at all.

That evening, I toured the city in my dusty car with its alien license plates, driving through the empty university—there were runners on the track and readers on the library steps, but schools are always strangely still, almost destitute, during the hottest weeks of the year—to look at the buildings Nina had described, the places she remembered from her college days. Afterwards I stopped at a pizza parlor. It was cool inside and the smell was wonderful, and the woman behind the counter was very friendly when I ordered. I enjoyed sitting and staring, almost blankly, through the big front window at the quiet street, fiercely lit by the midsummer sun, dropping down on the horizon. I realized I was unnaturally relaxed; I was taking advantage of a chance bubble in my life to become, for once, totally unconcerned. The day seemed poised, as if waiting for some event, and it made me think of a story I'd heard about the city from a friend who'd passed through. He'd seen a circus parade from the counter of a coffee shop; the old men around him had watched together in passive agitation, genuinely astonished, though they were plainly the kind who made it a habit to be surprised by nothing. "Elephants on Main Street," one of them had said, shaking his head. "I never thought I'd see the day."

My dinner was getting cold but I sat for several minutes, staring out the window. "Everything all right, sir?" the woman called to me.

"Fine," I answered. "Smells great." Having said that, I was obliged to interrupt my trance and lift up a piece. It was very good—I'd remembered for once to ask for olives—and I finished the first piece, then had another and started a third, eating quickly, as content to stare at the street while chewing my food as while sitting motionless, aware as I was that for the first time in months I was dining alone.

The next morning I slept late, knowing there was no reason not to. It was another bright day. The room depressed me terribly as I opened my eyes, admitting I was awake, and got up to use the toilet. For the next five minutes it was awful; I almost wished I'd called Nick, who Nina had said owned a big house in a sleepy town, half an hour from the city, and would jump at a chance to put me up. If I had I might have been sitting at a messy kitchen table in the sun, eating oranges and English muffins and watching Nick's latest as she sat in his T-shirt on the other side, wondering if she knew he never stayed with anyone for very long, instead of staring at the veneered desk with postcards of the motel and an area guide, and the television bolted to the wall, and the cracked parking lot outside the curtained window.

I thought of calling Nina, then remembered she would already be out of the house. There were good books in my suitcase, and Sunday papers with sports and comics for sale nearby; I even had work to do, and there was a neat and sunny coffee shop attached to the motel, with large tables where I could spread out my memos and figures and graphs. But I felt vaguely anxious, almost panicked, at the thought of the time that stretched in front of me. I wanted to be at home, where I knew what the choices were, where I had such a backlog of both business and pleasure that there was never any question of being at loose ends.

As I left the room I remembered something else my wife had told me. I went back and found her note in the zippered pocket of my case. Below the columns of names and phone numbers, with a brief note beside each, it said: "Dear Honey, you must go to get a bird while you are there. You will be sorry if you don't. Go to Sam's Birdland, on the strip road by the airport, and order a chicken dinner, with extra sauce (on the side). You should also ask for a large ice water. Do not fail to do this." A bird, she'd explained, was a deep-fried half chicken with hot barbecue sauce on white bread, and a serving of macaroni salad. She and her friends had often "gone to get a bird," at times on a weekly basis. I'd reminded her that I ate barbecued chicken all the time—most recently with her, at the Dixie Diner—but she'd said a bird was different, and had even tried to talk me into bringing one back for her, until I'd convinced her it would never make it home intact in the summer heat.

I decided I would get a bird before seeing Sallie. There was time for me to have a cup of coffee, drive to Sam's for lunch, and get to her house by two, even if I had trouble finding it. At the last moment I remembered to take another shirt with me, just in case.

Finding the restaurant turned out to be easy, but when I got there it was shut up tight. I'd known from the map which strip road Nina meant and it was exactly as I'd imagined it: grass fields and chain-link fences and small planes on the airport side, with wind socks and old hangars just past the Cessnas and the main airport a mile beyond that, airliners shimmering from afar, and on the other side single-story offices and outlets and banquet halls, and a McDonald's and a Wendy's, and a miniature golf course and driving range, and then Sam's Birdland. When I saw there were no cars floating on the smooth asphalt pond around the glass and brick pavilion, I realized it was silly to expect a barbecued chicken place to be open on Sunday morning. The sign on the door said "Sun 11 am–11 pm," but there was no one inside, and no sign of life.

As I sat in the car with my feet on the pavement, trying to decide what to do, a young couple arrived in a convertible sports car. "It's closed," I called to them as they rolled up and stopped.

"Is that so," said the man. They got out and peered through the door. "Jimmy is gonna be so disappointed," she said. "The game and everything."

"Screw Jimmy," the man said. "He coulda come himself." He turned to me. "You know what time it opens?" he asked. I shrugged and shook my head. He seemed to understand then that he was dealing with an idiot, someone who would sit endlessly in an empty parking lot by the airport. "Come on," he said to the woman. She smiled at me as they got in and roared away.

I started to walk over to the golf place to see if anybody knew when Sam's would open, or why it might be closed. As I passed the edge of the miniature golf course—it was a small, crowded one, the kind where the holes are packed tightly together, a curve in one forcing a curve in the next, but there were several interesting ornaments and obstacles, including a crouching tiger who ate the ball and passed it out through the tip of his tail—I thought I might play a round or two if Sam's didn't open. I walked along the edge of a low whitewashed building until I turned into an open, tiled foyer that separated it from another wing beyond, with patio furniture pushed up against the walls. It made me think of a rural guest house in a tropical country; I looked for a ceiling fan, slowly whirling.

On the other side was the driving range. It was a green oasis after the barren airport plateau. At least ten people were lined up, close to the building and the paved walk that ran along it, with their clubs and visors and buckets of balls, each placing a small white sphere on the rubber tee, standing and wiggling or looking out over the range, then raising the club and, with a grunt and a whack, driving the ball toward the distant yardage signs. The sounds were continuous, but my eye tried to resolve the timing of a dozen individuals into one coordinated cycle of tee, settle, drive. Some of the balls arced very high; others hooked and sliced, or on occasion bounced not far from the tee. One man, short and broad with dark skin and very black hair, was hitting powerful line drives, straight and true, so fast I heard them whiz.

A teenager was sitting at a small counter set in the wall of the building. Behind him I saw an office, with a telephone and a typewriter and some ledgers. I asked if he knew when Sam's would open and he said he didn't.

"Are they usually open at this time on Sundays?" I asked.

"I guess so," he said. I saw the short dark man turn and look at us before driving another ball.

"Do you have a phone book?" I asked. "I'd like to call to see if there's anyone there."

"Either that or I have a menu here somewhere," he said. "Give me a second." As I turned to watch the small man hit his rockets, he coiled and swung and launched a truly majestic one—I strained to follow it though the air as the sun leaked into my eyes from the side—that carried all the way to the 225 sign and, as we both stood waiting, hit it with an audible thump. "Yeah," the man said under his breath.

The boy came back with a menu from Sam's, but as I took it from him the dark man turned around. He was wearing old shorts and a paint-stained undershirt. "One o'clock," he said. "He opens at one o'clock on Sundays in the summer."

"That's what I wanted to know," I said. "Thank you." He grinned. His shirt was soaked, and he was clearly tired but very happy with himself. He looked as though he'd worked hard over many years for the right to drive golf balls on Sunday morning.

"You eat there, Dag?" asked the teenager.

"All the time," said Dag. "Every day."

"Is it good?" I asked.

Dag grinned again, or kept on grinning; he'd never stopped. "I eat there a lot," he said. "I love chicken. I love birds. If it isn't good, I guess I've lost my judgment entirely." He looked from one to the other of us. "You have to have a taste for that kind of chicken," he said.

One o'clock was early enough for me to have my meal, but what would I do for more than an hour? I thought of asking Dag to teach me to hit golf balls—he was already at work again, his back all sweat and concentration—but I was afraid he would resent me, or refuse me. "Thanks," I said to the teenager, and he smiled and nodded. "Thank you, Dag," I said as I walked past him. He was between drives. "My pleasure," he said, lifting another ball out of the bucket, squinting at 250.

I walked out and past the miniature golf course. The only players were an old man and two children, a girl and a boy of startlingly different appearance. I assumed at first that the fair girl belonged to the man, that the brown boy was a friend of hers, but when I saw how he treated them exactly the same—holding them from behind to help them with their putters, touching them lovingly when they ran up to him—I knew they were both his grandchildren. Though I resisted, it moved me to see them in that setting. As I'd wanted to join Dag, I thought it would do me good to be among them, but I knew it wouldn't work; they were having such fun, laughing and talking, but to me they were pathetic, helpless and unsuspecting; I would come to them like a curse.

I watched for a while, enjoying their game, listening to the jets land and take off and thinking about my grandfather when he lived alone in Florida, across from the restaurant with the painted mule by the door, then set out to find something to occupy me until Sam's opened. I drove miles down the road, but the only real possibility was a huge bowling alley, the parking lot full of cars, the lanes certainly crowded with skilled bowlers who knew each other well.

As I went even further south and then north again, I remembered the discussions I'd had with Nina about sending a wedding invitation to Sallie. I had been optimistic, Nina reluctant. "She won't come," she'd told me. "Will you be glad you tried?" I'd asked. "What difference does it make?" she'd said, restraining impatience. "Don't think I haven't made the effort to be in touch with her, because I have. She never answers anything and she never sends anything. You might as well be shoving your letters down a hole."

After two or three attempts, I had stopped trying to find out whether she really wanted Sallie there or not; we would send an invitation, I'd decided, and wait for her reply. Nina had been relieved by this, even more so when the deadline had passed with no card from Sallie. I'd tried to suggest that she call, but before five words were out of my mouth she'd said, "Look, my friend, I told you what would happen, and I was right, and I'm extremely certain I don't want to do anything further about it. Understand?" Sallie had not come to the wedding, and had not been mentioned again until I'd told Nina about my trip.

Finding nothing to fill my time, I ended up at the Wendy's, drinking more coffee I didn't want and feeling it sour my stomach, reading an old mystery I'd discovered on the floor of the car. It seemed like a silly way to spend the day, so I went back to Sam's and read a few more pages in the parking lot, then put my seat back for a quick nap. I woke up at five past one, but Sam wasn't there. No one had arrived by one-fifteen or half-past; no one else had come looking, like the couple I'd met before. All my information was faulty. I gave up and drove away, discouraged, wondering if I would ask someone where else I might go, or find a way to try Sam's again before leaving town.

As I neared Sallie's house the sidewalks were progressively more littered, the structures more weathered and deteriorated, though nothing actually looked ruined or abandoned. I was glad, when I turned onto her street, to see well-kept homes and neatly mowed lawns, with flowers planted along the edges. It looked like a happy block, if not hugely prosperous. Her house was small but attractive; it was freshly painted white, with deep blue and gray trim and odd, many-paned windows. Behind it I could see a shaded yard.

She was standing in the doorway, on the other side of the screen, as I parked the car at the curb and came up the walk; indistinct as she was, I was aware at first of the feminine lines of her body, in a tank top and skirt, but not of her face. When she pushed open the screen door I saw that it was lined and much older than Nina's, though they were the same age. She smiled at me.

"It's good to see you," she said. "You look like a very nice man."

"People have told me that," I said, "but never so quickly."

She laughed and relaxed slightly and gave me her hand, which I shook. "Come in," she said. We went through a short hall and stood at the end of a room lined with books, a big leather couch along the far side. There were a few framed reproductions on the walls.

"Books and comfortable furniture," I said. "Just what I like." She glanced at me.

"The living room," she said with a gesture. "And here," she went on, turning and going through a doorway, "is the kitchen. And here," she finished, as she opened the refrigerator and took out a pitcher, "is the lemonade." She put the pitcher on the table, then reached into a cupboard and brought out two tall plastic tumblers. She placed these neatly by the pitcher and looked at me with remarkably evident curiosity, her head cocked. I tried to meet her gaze but was embarrassed; instead I looked at the windowsill, on which were arranged several small potted plants, and through the glass to the back yard.

"Should we sit outside?" she asked. "I don't think it's too hot."

"I'd like that," I said, but we continued to stand there, watching each other. Sallie had her hands on her hips; she didn't appear to mind my eyes on whatever part of her I chose to examine. I realized I had the advantage of her, because I knew a good deal about her and she knew nothing about me. It was an obvious asymmetry, and in fact as I thought about it her look turned self-conscious, and she lowered her eyes and seemed to shake her head. "We'd better sit down," she said. She picked up the pitcher and I took the glasses and she led me through the back door to a flagstoned patio, with three painted metal chairs and a table of the same type, but from another set.

What I knew was that she'd slept with women all her life, except for a short and unhappy marriage; that she and my wife had been roommates for several years, close friends of youth, and—in an experiment for Nina, an adventure easily come to and easily abandoned—briefly lovers; that she had subsequently, perhaps on the rebound, acquired a girlfriend whom Nina had considered shallow, vain, and thoroughly unappealing, though very pretty; that she didn't eat tomatoes, or corn, and loved to play basketball; that she had wept freely every time Nina made love to her; that she had accepted money from her parents, but had sometimes written out a check for the amount they'd sent, weeks later, and returned it to them.

Sallie poured out lemonade and handed it to me, then poured for herself and sat down. Though I continued to wonder at the age in her face, and the way it made her look worn out and resigned, I noticed again the neat and attractive shape of her, including her excellent calves and thighs, emerging from her cotton skirt. I wanted to avoid this persistent distraction; under the circumstances it seemed ludicrous as well as ungracious.

"You have a lovely house," I told her. "I envy you. On such a quiet, pretty little street."

"I like it," she said. "I spend most of my time here." She took a long drink of her lemonade. "I do a lot of my work at home and I live alone, so I have a lot of silent time in the house. I feel loved by it. I'm very lucky." She smiled again, a genuine smile, I thought. "I'm sorry if I'm too sentimental about a building," she said. "I started life as a poor person. I still can't get used to the idea that I've actually earned a house of my own."

"I understand very well," I said.

As we talked further, about her job and mine, about how she and Nina had found each other through a notice taped to a laundromat wall, I thought of my wife, stretching and smiling and beckoning to me, calling me by private names; I tried to imagine what had passed between them. Could they have been so intimate? When they sat together, drinking lemonade—not here, but in some yard a few miles distant, attractive young women on a summer day—had Sallie been as she now was, in her pink top and white skirt and sneakers, back straight, hands on the armrests, eyes clear but with something in reserve, or had she opened herself, leaning into the sun with limbs sprawled, watching her companion, sighing with the satisfaction of being near her?

Sallie was telling me about a kitten they'd had, how she'd been trapped inside a wall and rescued by the fire department, when a boy walked into the yard. That he was her son was obvious, though they weren't enormously like each other; it was in the way he looked at her and at me, and the way she turned to him when she heard his step.

"Hi, darling," she said with pleasure as he came to her. She kissed him on the cheek and took his hands. He was ten or eleven; Nina had certainly known all about him, but she hadn't told me. "This is Henry, who is married to someone I used to know very well," Sallie said. "Henry, this is Benjamin." He turned to me and smiled, then faced her again.

"I rode my bike over, Ma," he said. "Do you want to come riding with me?"

Her look asked me to indulge his disregard for my presence, but also showed pride in his attachment to her. "I can't, sweetheart," she told him. "I have a guest. Henry came a long way to see me. Can we go another time?" She kissed him again. "Ben lives nearby with his father," she explained. "He loves to surprise me with visits."

I expected the child to be disappointed and upset and I was prepared to have it made plain that I was coming between them, but he took it well. He had honestly wanted her company, I saw, but there was also satisfaction in having asked. "Okay," he said. "Can I take a doughnut?"

"If I have any," she said. "Don't go too far alone," she called after him as he entered the house. "I won't," he yelled. We heard a cabinet opening and closing, and the slam of the screen door in front.

"I see you're very close," I said.

"We are," she said, shutting her eyes, as if she'd decided there was too much to look at. "We are."

We sat quietly for a few minutes—I heard a bird calling, and a neighbor cutting his grass, and thought how nice it was that we could so soon be silent together—until Sallie suggested that we drive around town. She seemed eager to show me the sights. Though I'd convinced myself the day before that, despite my Nina's past, the city meant nothing to me, it seemed only courteous to go along. I liked the way she quickly took a small wallet and her keys and left the house, without the fussy preparation of many women I knew; as I followed her to her car, which she insisted on taking—"You're the guest," she said, "what kind of host would I be if I let you drive?"—I watched the sway of her skirt and realized, uneasily, that I was looking forward to sharing the smaller space of the front seat with her, to being that much closer.

As it turned out she had a very old Dodge, exactly the car I would have expected her to have; it was clean and neatly kept, with a bench seat, and there was nothing between us after we'd put on our seat belts but smooth blue vinyl. It started instantly, and she grinned and put her hand on the dashboard before backing out of the driveway and heading toward the river.

Sallie showed me a number of things that afternoon, points of general interest as well as places that had figured in her life and Nina's, but I'd forgotten most of them by the time they were out of sight. Though she was articulate and funny as she told me about their parties and predicaments and jobs and disasters, and about her hometown, she couldn't hold my attention; my curious relaxation of the day before was back, washing over me, making her car a comfort, her voice a balm, the tour not an event but a context within which I could be alone, a single point, and think little or not at all.

After looking at an apartment they'd lived in, above a cocktail bar and across from a used book store, we turned down a street in a leafy neighborhood. At its end we faced a large gabled house, with a broad front porch. On the porch was a woman in a wicker chair, and next to her, hanging from the rafters, utterly still in the breezeless

air, was a huge American flag. For a moment, as the car rolled to
a stop, we looked at each other. Her tranquility was as profound as
mine, her worries as unreal; we were content to see each other
directly, though we had nothing to convey.

"Nina did love chicken," Sallie said as she showed me a diner
they'd liked. "She'd eat it any place and any time."

"She told me all about the birds here," I said. She turned, and I
realized I hadn't spoken for a while. "They sound wonderful."

"Do you like that kind of food?" she asked.

"I do," I said. "I like almost anything." We were nearing the
downtown area; it was empty and quiet, in a summer Sunday way.
"Nina told me to get a bird," I said, "and I tried today, but the
restaurant was closed."

"You did? Where did you go?"

"Sam's Birdland," I said.

"Near the airport?"

"Right by it."

"Yes," she said, nodding, "we went there a lot. I haven't been in
years."

She pointed out the doll museum—a wealthy woman had left a
huge sum for the care of her collection, though Sallie didn't know
the details—and drove me past the Conservatory, then asked, "Can
I take you to get a bird right now? I'm sure we can find a place."

"That's all right," I said. "I'm not hungry."

"But it's a shame you didn't get one," she said. "I'd hate for you
to go away without trying one, especially if you were looking forward
to it." She glanced at me as we waited for a traffic light. "It's
something I'd like to do for you."

"I may try again tomorrow," I said. "I'm very happy as I am."
She was quiet, and I had a sudden vision: I wasn't going to have
chicken with her, though it seemed the most natural thing in the
world. "It's very kind of you," I said, "but I couldn't eat now."

"I understand," she said. "It's so hot."

We talked not at all as we drove to the house. I was embarrassed, knowing I'd been all sorts of things I was proud not to be, happy that no one else had seen it. I questioned my reasons for calling her in the first place, and tried to smile, and to keep from saying anything to make it worse.

"Please come in for coffee," she said, very firmly, as she pulled into the driveway and shut off the engine. I nodded. I thought she was making a final gesture before sending me on my way, so she could feel at peace about wishing me gone, but as soon as we were inside and had taken two steps toward the living room she turned and put her hand on my arm.

"Look," she said, "I've enjoyed getting to know you. I don't have anything on for this evening, and from what you've told me you don't either. Why don't you stay and have dinner with me?" We were very near each other, and despite the heat of the day I thought I could feel the warmth of her body. "I have a spare room, and I hate to think of you sleeping at that motel when you could be here. Later you could get your things, and spend the night."

I was pleased that despite myself I'd earned her good intentions. Then I looked in her eyes and saw loneliness and pride, and something else I recognized. I felt longing in her touch.

Though I'd pursued her all day, within myself, it frightened me. She was very appealing as she looked at me and it was shockingly easy to imagine myself inside her, grasping her hips and thighs as I took my satisfaction; whatever pleasure she might find in the form of my body, in the touching of my skin and bone, would be enhanced by the novelty, by the years that had passed since she'd known it last.

Even as I pictured her on the sheets I was backing away. "It's a generous offer," I said, "but I don't think so." As I spoke I saw her weakness, how she was barely holding on; I felt the weight of an enforced independence that went back forever. I had to refuse her, not out of decency or fidelity to Nina, but because we were nothing to our pains and our failings, because disappointment was so likely, because there was so little to be done.

Sallie dropped her hand and I fled down the path, ashamed, regretting everything, knowing it was impossible, beyond us both. We could have come briefly together and found our comfort, but the next morning, that very night, we would have wondered if it had really happened; we would have been ghosts to each other, passing visions in a mirror, accidents remembered only for their names.

# · Acts
# of
# Contrition

IF he didn't care enough to do anything about it, there was no point
in feeling sorry. That was what his father had told him. His father
had insisted, often, that the expression of regret was usually a pretense, a front for shame and the desire to avoid it, or at best an
insincere, reflexive response to another's pain, routinely trained into
children because it made things more pleasant. "I feel bad about it,"
he would say, and his father would ask, "Do you actually feel badly,"
emphasizing the second syllable just enough to include the gram-
matical correction in the lesson, "or are you afraid we will think
poorly of you if you don't?" This had been part of their relationship
from the beginning of his memory until his father's death.

"Don't make light of the suffering of others for your own con-
venience," his father would say. "Don't claim to share in that suffering when it means nothing to you. Don't clog up the world with
manufactured sorrow, it's in bad enough shape as it is. Say it truth-
fully or don't say it at all."

"I *am* sorry for what I did," Oscar would insist. "I do feel badly.
Don't you believe me?"

"Possibly," his father would say, and then, depending on the
circumstances, he would propose some substantial but reasonable

step that might be taken to address the situation. If Oscar had, out of meanness, failed to invite an unpopular classmate to a party, his father might suggest that Oscar take the other child out for ice cream, or spend an afternoon at his house. If Oscar had seen a family yelled at as they walked past a storefront by drunken teenagers because they were black, and felt he had been wrong not to involve himself, his father might raise the possibility of his walking through a black neighborhood until someone yelled at him, to find out first-hand what it was like, or of going to the offices of a civil rights organization and volunteering his time.

What continued to amaze Oscar, long after the last of these scenes had been played out, was the way his father had never seemed to care about his reasons for not taking the suggestion, for doing nothing. Oscar certainly knew the difference between "I'm afraid," and "I'm too young to do that," and "I don't see the point in it," and "I don't care enough to take that risk, to go to that kind of trouble," but at times his father appeared not to.

"Stop saying you're sorry, then," his father would instruct him, dropping the same words, heavily, on Oscar's explanation or excuse, whatever it might be, regardless of Oscar's upset or confusion, "and go on to something productive. You might think about what you'll do next time." For years he wondered why he could never recall a single instance of his having acted on what his father had said, until he decided one sleepless night that when there really was something to be done, something that made sense, that would help, he always did it quite naturally, by himself, with no need of his father's advice.

"He thinks I'm dishonest," Oscar remembered saying to his mother, following a long discussion about a small task he'd promised his father he would do and had then forgotten. It had been a very bitter evening. "He actually accused me of lying to him when I tried to apologize."

"I'm sure he didn't, dear," his mother had said. "He knows you're very truthful. He's very proud of you that way."

"What would you call 'I acknowledge your token of regret,'"
he'd asked, "a vote of confidence?"

"Perhaps he felt you had something more to say," she'd suggested.
Another thing that astonished him was that he'd continued to
return to his father, over and over, with his guilts and repentances.
As long as his father was alive, no crisis of obligation or confidence
was complete without this consultation, though it never yielded
anything to speak of and in fact dominated and diminished the
happier elements of their time together, of which there were many.
It was an unalterable need they shared equally, and in his clearest
moments Oscar knew they would have been lost without it. He had
never described this aspect of their relationship to anyone because
in doing so he would have branded himself as victim, or abuser, or
possibly both, and done the same for his father; it would have
sounded like a wounded antagonism, limping along, instead of the
rewarding friendship it generally was.

He was at times outraged to discover that, having abandoned his
intention of making amends or reversing himself in some difficult
situation, because he knew it wouldn't change anything and might
in any case be misunderstood by or even damaging to the intended
object of his reconsideration, he spoke in his father's voice. But never
until he had finally and irrevocably surrendered the chance to fix
what he'd broken. After a decade of displaying a repetitive inability
to get beyond a certain stage with women, and of deep political and
philosophical confusion, out of which he chose friends of wildly
varying attitude and station in life, he came to understand that his
father had given him, intentionally or not, a near-perfect mechanism
for denying, when he wanted to, the sense and purpose of ever doing
anything. He didn't blame his father for the inclination—like anyone
else he had reason enough to drop things to the ground, to walk
away from trouble—but he felt helpless to resist the capacity, and
puzzled endlessly over his apparent betrayal by the only hero he'd

ever had; he felt, almost, that his father had put a loaded gun in his hand.

In the hallway of his apartment, on the wall, he kept a photograph of his father as a young man, as an intern at the hospital, wearing rubber gloves and a smock and holding a tiny infant up, as if to display it. To Oscar, the smile in the picture encompassed all the joy, all the gaiety he'd tried to coax out of his father over the years. His pleasures were his father's pleasures, his triumphs shared as well, but his father had never seemed to have any that were truly his own, except for that one moment, in the delivery room, beside himself with satisfaction, holding the baby Oscar in his arms, before the world, for everyone to see.

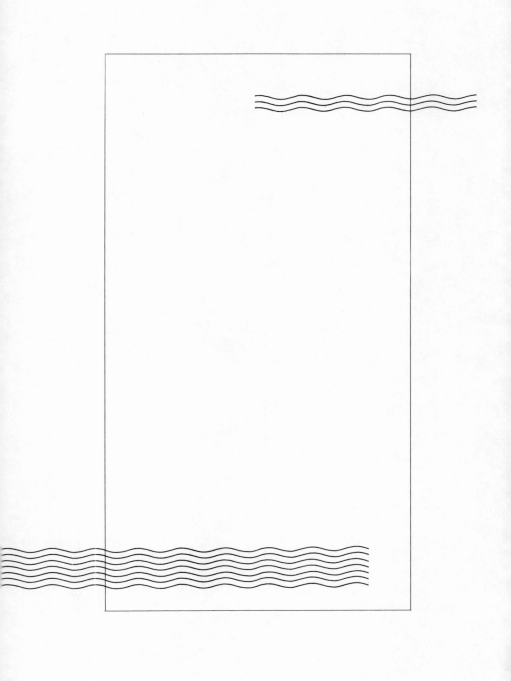

# · Detail,
# of Rock
# and Stream

SOME distance from the house, at a bend in the creek, there was
a place at which I often stopped. I usually stayed for less than a
minute, and I rarely sat down; it was enough to stand and watch
the water. The stream was suddenly wider and shallower, and there
were stones strewn across its bed, so that rapids were created in a
small, confined way, almost like an exhibit at a museum or a habitat
in a zoo but energetic and real, throwing spray, leaping and rushing,
transforming the flow for thirty or forty feet, ending as abruptly as
they began.

On the other side—a pebble's toss away—was a narrow bank
and the face of a large glacial boulder. It seemed to have been there
forever. Parts of it were exposed, parts covered with moss or
overhung with roots. It was very unlike the water, completely still,
but I knew it was active too: moss grew and withered, roots length-
ened and thickened, the rock itself had been born and would crumble, and eventually fall to pieces.

This was a place I loved, I found; I smiled when I thought of
my stream, from a distance, and when I came near. Its turbulent
waters soothed and welcomed me. It never faltered or hesitated, and
I fiercely admired this constancy; I wanted to surrender to its cer-

tainty of purpose, its steady confidence, its tranquillity and complex strength. I wanted to throw myself into it, and be swept away.

Lydia didn't understand my attachment. To her it was a pleasant spot, pretty and unremarkable, admired for a few minutes on our first walk along the path but not after that, because she had seen it. Instead she had questions; she wanted to know how the path had been laid out, and wondered who had arranged for it to loop around, almost doubling back on itself, to meet the river, leading right to the small bluff on the bank that overlooked the white water and the rocky face. She thought it might have been a child, one who spent a lot of time alone in the woods and visited special places, a thorough and determined child but very private, even secretive. When the house was made part of the colony, she said, one of the first guests had stumbled on the traces and followed them, telling the next person, who passed it on in turn until it came to us. "Don't waste any time getting out into the forest," Marian had said as she left us, unfamiliar keys in our hands, surrounded by our suitcases in the small front hall. "The path starts at the back corner of the yard. You can't help but stay on it. It makes a lovely walk."

We often talked as we went through the woods. This was Lydia's preference, not mine, but I could indulge her; I found the silence I needed when I walked alone, which I did every day, on the path or to the main house, or along the road. She was cheerful and easy when not at work, abandoning with her brushes and paints the woman of violence and bitter reproach, of frightening shapes and combinations, who so upset me that I never went to see her unless invited, and went cautiously even then. It was different for me. I was always involved with whatever I was doing, never entirely away from my desk; this annoyed her because it meant—she thought it meant—that my attention was never wholly hers. I was careful, even fussy, moving in small steps, fearful of hexing myself; she was a force of nature, a tide. I believed I was the kind of author you might read about in a book, while she—on some days she returned to the house with a terrible grimace, marched though to the back porch and slammed the door behind her, emerging later, sunny again, for dinner—was the painter you would imagine in an empty studio, or invent for a movie, or meet in a dream.

We talked about beauty but we used different languages; I took it where I found it, she conjured it like a demon. There were days when I envied her painfully. I was embarrassed by my timidity, my qualifications, my imperceptible changes of direction. Whatever she was, Lydia knew how to be; I came to myself by accident, unsure of what I would find. Lydia knew she was a woman because she looked just like one; she knew she was an artist because when she saw what she'd done, she wept and wanted to shriek or run, or to grip her knees with whitened hands. "It makes my heart beat faster," she said.

There was much we shared, and much we didn't; we were close but it was a fragile closeness, almost arbitrary. It disturbed me to be at odds with her, to live in mystery, to see the spaces between us and the questioning looks. I found her bracelet on the bed and asked, Whose is this? She was with me through the day. I worked at my desk and tried to put her from me; I wondered, endlessly, if she was there on the page; I felt a sudden panic as I sat, my pen waiting to mark the moment's changes, and forgot the words while I struggled to remember what she'd dressed in that morning, or eaten the night before, so I could calm myself and go on. I described and explained her to my parents, to my brothers, to the people I admired as I walked my walks, and I asked why it concerned me, why I needed to ask at all, when I was productive, even happy, when things were going so well.

Sometimes I felt she was years and lives ahead of me, that she had learned to leave the world entirely, to not know or care whether her paintings had to do with what was outside her walls. Sometimes I saw on her face an awareness that chilled me, because it started and ended with her, and would never see the day.

"This is a first for us," said Max Kuroda as he poured our wine. "We've never had a couple here, working independently, living together." We were at the weekly gathering. He was a small man with a wide face and wavy, shiny black hair; his coat and tie were conspicuous, and begged our questions.

"We can't be so unusual," said Lydia, sipping from her glass.

"No," said Kuroda, "there are others like you—perhaps fewer than you think—but we've not been honored by any in the past." He saw me examining his suit and smiled, and tugged with his left hand at the lapel. "I met with some locals this afternoon," he told me. "This was for them."

"They don't wear suits, do they?" I asked.

He laughed. "Of course not," he said. "They spend most of the day covered in cow shit. But they need to know I'm not one of the artists. This makes me someone they understand."

"I wouldn't have guessed it," I said.

Lydia glanced at me. "What an unusual life you lead, Mr. Kuroda," she said to him. She was so charming, I thought, and so genuine; I despaired of ever rising to her level of grace. "You speak for us."

"I keep you dry and well fed, if that," he said.

On some days, as I stood at the bend in the stream, and listened to my favorite sound, and watched the smooth, full shape of the water as it poured over the rounded orange stone near the opposite shore, I thought of Lydia as she sometimes was when she made love to me: determined, carefully metered, almost relentless in her gradual but steady movement toward the end. "Darling, darling, darling," she would whisper to me. Like the rushing water, my lover had the courage to repeat herself. "Darling, darling, darling," the water said to me as I turned my back and walked away down the path. "Here I am, here I am, here I am."

I asked Faber, a sculptor Lydia knew from the city, if he had seen her work. I thought they might have compared notes. They

weren't friends but they weren't rivals; she respected him, and had
been pleased to hear he would be at the colony too.

"I haven't," he told me. "What is she working on?"

"I have no idea," I said.

"Do you talk about the work?" he asked.

"We talk about working," I said, "but not about the work."

We were sitting in the sun, in big wooden armchairs set in front
of the main house beside the driveway, chairs that had an unused
look. We had discovered, without saying it, that we shared an enthusiasm for being out by the door, near the action, such as it was:
Kuroda chatting with the letter carrier, the dog rolling and biting
its haunches, the cooks signing for vegetables and chickens and
cartons of toilet paper. We had never planned to meet, to be there
together, but somehow we'd managed to arrange it; I sat for no
more than forty minutes, three or four times a week, and Faber was
usually there when I was, an unlikely coincidence.

" 'It loved to happen,' " said Faber.

"Excuse me?"

"Marcus Aurelius," he said. *Meditations.*

I shifted in my seat.

"That's what occurs to me," he said, "when I think of your Lydia."

Not long afterwards she came back to the house, around seven
o'clock—on a midsummer evening, when it seemed as if the light
would never end—and said, "Play time. Are you through?"

"Yes," I said. I looked up from my book. "Are you?"

"I'm through, through, through," she said. "I'm never going back.
Let's take a walk."

"Aren't you hungry?" I asked. "There's a cheese in the icebox."
She shook her head. "How about a shower? Or a nap?"

"Let's go for a walk," she said. When I paused in the kitchen,
she pulled on my hand.

We walked together. The forest that evening was everything I
imagined when I pictured it as I sat at my desk: rich, dense, deep,

full of smells and dampness, made of rustlings and diggings and changing situations. When I thought about where I would most like to be, the setting in which I most wanted to work, I dreamed of the barren, open hills and fields of northern Scotland, which I had never seen, the moving sunlight through the cloud-scattered sky, the tree in the distance and the unobstructed wind. But when I touched the world that held a place for me—the reality in which I lived—I knew it was more like the forest, surrounding me, denying me my purity and my light.

Lydia, for once, seemed moved by the woods, even awed. She held my arm with both of hers as we walked, and looked up at the leaves. "It goes forever," she said. "Does it have an end?"

We moved quietly and not very quickly; she was small and child-like, as she'd been only late at night, or in rooms far from home. I felt constrained, as I touched her, and wondered if it was something new or just my familiar attachment to silence, calling on me at a difficult time.

When we reached the rapids she sat on one of the large rocks by the shore, facing the small open area, her left to the water. I sat across from her, the stream on my right. Though I'd chosen this arrangement I was puzzled by it, and embarrassed; I glanced at the boulder's dark face, off of which the water echoed, and was dismayed to have her there, and to wish her gone.

"It's not going well," said Lydia. "It's not going well at all." She sat with her hands on her legs, above the knees, her feet spread apart as if about to rise. "This is so difficult. It isn't what it seems. I'm supposed to be free, but I feel so required."

I was saddened, preparing for loss. She was a pleasure alien to me, a reward to which I wasn't entitled, a source of warmth and substance that I didn't have to grope for, to seek out haltingly, to measure with one eye and ignore with the other for fear she would melt away, or crumble to dust. She asked me to be what I knew I was not; feeling the weight of my questions and doubts I shrugged, and refused to entertain them.

"I never had this kind of trouble before," she said. "It isn't any good. I dread that awful studio, and trying and trying. I feel stupid and spiteful. I want to throw out all the canvases." She looked at the creek and leaned slightly to one side, smiling as if she had just discovered it. "I want to go away with you, honey. I don't want to be a painter anymore."

She stood and took off her shirt. "Love me," she said. My chest ached; she was a forest sprite, her hair flowing, a lovely darkness; she might have coaxed the leaves down from the trees, caused the breeze to quicken, moved the earth. She asked something of me, and I wanted to refuse; she was open to me, perhaps as she had always been, but urgently. I could not leave her to stand, unsuccored.

She came to me and sat in the dirt at my feet, rested her head on my knee, stroked me with her hand. I reached out with mine, listening to the water, as if I could hear it cross and cover and divide around every pebble, no matter how small and how round; I saw her perfect breast, and felt her shoulder with my fingers, which rested firmly on her but were known, by both of us, to be elsewhere. She stroked me and wept as I embraced both her and my torrent, my flood, but within myself, in a hidden place, surprised and awakened by my essential solitude, and the knowledge of what I had, what I needed, all I could do without.

# · Cheaters
# and Liars,
# Robbers
# and Fools

WHEN she was a girl, coming home from school, she hurried to the kitchen to see what she could find. Disturbing nothing, she chose what wouldn't be missed: four crackers, eleven grapes, a slice of cheese from the opened package. Some things went together, like a bagel half, from a bag of six or seven cut for brunch but never eaten, and knife-shavings of whipped butter from the waxed cardboard tub; others made strange combinations. She took a plate from the cupboard and arranged her collection, carefully, as in a photograph in a magazine: bright colors in the center, others running in a circle around the edge, or radiating in lines.

Carrying the plate to her room, to the bedside table, she propped herself with pillows and read and ate. On some afternoons she rationed herself—one olive or wafer or cherry tomato for every two pages, or every four—and on others she ate quickly and apprehensively, as if her mother might arrive home suddenly and surprise her in her indulgence. This almost happened twice, and each time, when she heard the car, she was able to put the remaining food into her mouth and force it down, then hide the plate under the bed before her mother came to her room.

In this time of her life she rarely has the patience for elaborate snacks or meals. She often thinks of the kitchen at home, of the books she read and of her room, perhaps occupied now by another child, daughter of the attractive couple that bought the house from her parents, after they divorced, during her first semester at the university. Usually these thoughts are characterized by the detachment that dominates her waking hours, but at intervals it hurts to remember her room, and she takes time to cry and sometimes to call out the names of the cats and dogs they had. Even as it happens she expects, briefly, that tears will lead to some semblance of cheerfulness, and a fresh start.

She isn't actually depressed, as she tells her affable assistant, who nods and seems to understand; she isn't really unhappy. She is mostly tired, and even that description of her problem—why not get some sleep, or see a doctor?—makes it more mysterious, more compelling than she wants it to be. She is tired of doing anything it might naturally occur to her to do, and she's tired of being tired, and of trying to figure out why; she doesn't want to explain, she doesn't want to take steps, she doesn't want to understand. She does, rarely, want more pleasure, even excitement, but these are far from her, and so unlikely to come nearer—she will do nothing to change her circumstances—that she accepts their absence in return for days without distress.

Just two things pull at her, like her skirt catching on a nail. Every so often, when walking to or from work, or sitting on her stool before opening the next carton of notebooks or stamp pads, or running by the river, she feels that a shimmering curtain, rolled up in the sky, is about to descend, almost but not entirely obscuring whatever is in front of her, and that when it rises again—after how long?—everything will be different, she will be the things she can almost imagine when she thinks of what everybody expected of her, of the false starts she made and the truer ones she thought of and never arrived at. Her lack of interest in what is called *her life* will disappear, will be barely remembered.

The second thing is that time is passing. She is still young, but even under the best of circumstances, even if she has an idea and makes a decision and displays great determination and even the ability to sacrifice, nothing she could choose to do with herself would take less than years. I don't own anything, she thinks. I have no assets. I have no substance.

When she was smaller, before junior high school and boys and the youth orchestra, she spent many of her days alone, reading on her bed, looking at television, sitting by the picture window and watching the street. Her mother felt she must have friends; she was sent to parties, signed up for activities, enrolled in groups until she wondered if she would ever have a peaceful hour. When the weather was good her mother sometimes ordered her to "go out and play." There were children of her age in the neighborhood; they didn't dislike her, but their concerns were not hers, and she had no place in their games. Usually, after watching them for a time, saying little, she wandered away and walked in the forest, looking for something of interest. Once she tried to climb trees. Another day she found the clean, dry skull of what she decided was a skunk. She stared up at the treetops (sometimes turning in a slow circle, hearing the wind and leaves), stooped or bent to see under bushes (but never touched them with her hands), tried hard to find the birds beautiful, inspiring. When she began to be aware of her own breathing, to feel each little patch of sunlight as it passed over her skin, she returned to the house and announced, through the screen door, that she'd been out long enough. If her mother did not think so, she might go back into the woods, or she might stand—though the door was unlocked— with her hands in front of her, watching her mother make dinner or talk on the telephone, until beckoned inside.

There are a number of men who show an interest in her. Several are difficult but some are nice, one in particular, who delivers for a wholesaler and seems so burly and large, in his dirty jeans and unkempt beard, so devil-may-care, but was once, she has been told, a mild, presentable head librarian in another town. She has been to lunch with him a few times, to dinner twice, and though she almost enjoys these outings—she imagines she would if something in her were adjusted, pushed aside or left ajar—and he hasn't pressed her, she thinks she sees something in his eyes, as if he were licking his lips on the inside, and is certain he is waiting for her to "open up" so he can begin to convince her to be his girlfriend and to marry him or, if she has misjudged him, to go to bed with him. When he asks her to have lunch with him she sometimes says no when she is free and bored and hungry, or yes when she wants to be alone. She doesn't know which of them she is keeping off-balance.

Her oldest friend, with whom she saw movies and bicycled and danced long ago, with whom she talks long-distance, always asks, sooner or later, about men. Naomi is easily beautiful, with large, high breasts and exceptional legs, and where she generates interest, Naomi brings down an urgent hysteria. The men are drawn; having seen her they *must meet her*, often going to great lengths. Naomi (who adapts to everything) accepts this elemental eagerness of men; it flows into her life; she is puzzled by women who don't know it as she does. When there are no men she doesn't worry. She is certain in her bones of an unlimited supply, stacked like cold cans in a soda machine, waiting to roll into her hand. To speak to Naomi about any man—the one she dates, a customer at the store, the young clerk at the town hall, a neighbor—would mean questions and no answers, and Naomi would be alarmed, saying, men are for having.

She supposes that anyone who knows about her marriage assumes she avoids men out of bitterness, hurt, or anger. She is a little bitter, and sometimes angry, but from the moment when she finally, completely, thoroughly stopped loving him or even caring about what happened to him—standing in their living room, he threw his textbook to the floor and called her a name, and she understood something she'd been reaching for for years—there has been no pain. He is so little in her thoughts that when her friends refer to him she often doesn't know whom they mean, and when she does think of him it doesn't upset her, although she is a little ashamed.

She takes long walks at night and feels cheated when she remembers how they walked together, not because she wants him or any man to be with her but because she feels she should have, at least, a few pleasant memories—walking together, favorite restaurants, adventures—to show for a marriage, no matter how it ended or what was said. She is honest enough to admit—to the wall, to the steering wheel, to the bus shelter near her house—that the lack of affect associated with her memories, not only of her ex-husband but of anything from her past, is abnormal, that there is a part of herself she is childishly refusing, a territory walled off, not shown on any maps. I have nothing to trade, she tells herself, and no one to trade with. Her dreams—which she carefully records in a little book bound in paisley that she keeps by her bed—are the drama in her life. She writes them down, first thing in the morning, and hardly thinks about them later, though she does sometimes return to a confused and complicated page from weeks before. One dream—she is standing on a dock or a shore, and a ship, with every person she ever knew (or imagined to be part of her life) hanging over the stern rail, waving, is slowly pulling away, so slowly that the time when it will be too distant for her to see the faces of the people, or the waving hands, is unimaginable—has stayed with her for months, comes to her during the day, wherever she happens to be, takes her breath away.

Her friends are kind; she favors those who talk about themselves and those who don't talk at all. She can't return to the days when she fed and cared for every intimacy with phone calls, with letters and arrangements, and is losing those who are easily hurt. Michele, who runs with her, is silent to the point of sullenness; Ray is painfully funny and full of weird theories and short-lived crises; with Sally she shops for clothes. When she thinks of the lunches and dinners with them, and the afternoon teas, she wonders if they know each other's names, whether they leave fingerprints on the forks and glasses; she remembers driving her English teacher's car and being stopped on a country highway by the local police, who explained that they had an all-points bulletin on the make and model she was driving, in the same color, with plates from the same state, but let her go even though the registration was not in her name, filling her with puzzlement as she slowly, nervously, put the car in gear and drove away, looking in the rearview mirror to see them switch off their flashing lights and turn down a side road, instantly lost in the trees.

It surprises her that she takes care of herself so well and so easily: paying the mortgage, changing the oil, returning the library books, calmly discussing with the couple next door the matter of the tree that has fallen, pulling down a section of fence. For weeks at a time her only satisfaction, her passion is checking the inventory, cleaning the kitchen, knowing exactly what is to be paid out and taken in during the next three months. I am old enough, she tells herself, to understand what must be done; no one need worry about me again. She would rather see the papers on the kitchen table, squared to the corners, than hear the phone ring; she would rather advise her assistant about where to buy wallpaper and sink fittings than turn, startled, on the street, to see a stranger walking toward her and calling her name.

When she was very small, her playmates joined her in her yard on a sunny summer afternoon. Her mother brought grape juice on a tray. They gathered at the concrete stoop outside the kitchen door, and when her mother had given them cups she stepped forward ahead of the others, holding hers out to be filled. As her mother started pouring she exclaimed, "I forgot! Guests go first!" and pulled her hand back. The grape juice poured onto the steps; her mother was very angry; she sent her friends away.

Sometimes, when she walks in the dark, she stamps her foot, then looks around to see if anyone is listening.

# · Willie

WILLIE had an inner office. When I went there I stood with my back to the door and he sat at his desk, looking past me, across the hall and through another office to the window there. I felt, enclosed by his walls, that I was in a submarine or some underground complex, perhaps as part of a test. He discussed his plans and gestured at the charts and tables I'd brought him and I glanced at the ventilation grill over his head, as if small ribbons fluttered there in the steady, undetectable breeze. It was always with relief that I turned to find daylight in the corridor, not that I was above ground after all, free to come and go, but that the building in which I spent a quarter of my week, a third of my waking time, was not really so limited and lifeless. Rather, there was something about Willie's corner of it that made me want the light.

Willie was earnest, even serious at times, but the decorations in his office were mostly fanciful. There were drawings by his children, of monsters and mixed-up animals and things that never happened, and movie stills and baseball pictures, and there were his Ansel Adams posters, fantastic scenes: strange shapes, vast distances, life unbridled, desolation triumphant. Half Dome at Yosemite—I remembered looking at it from across the valley, finding a glint of

56
·

metal two thirds of the way up the sheer, consuming face, hearing
that it was a climber who was not using ropes—and a frosty, mam-
moth peak, crags retreating into the mist and a winding river gleaming in the sun. And there were huge mesas in the southwest desert,
towering over the expanse around them, almost flaunting their bizarre, mythical presence, challenging the elemental joining of earth
and sky from which they could never have sprung. I knew from
books that they'd been there all along, buried under the sand, rising
slowly as the rain washed it away and down to the sea, but when
I looked at Willie's poster I thought they might have been created
by some power as a sort of lesson, a reminder that reality finds
endless combinations, some wholly beyond expectation and well out
of reach. To me they were icons of regret.

The first time I visited Willie—I don't think he came to my office
once, in all the months I worked with him—I sat in the chair by
the side of his desk while he explained his project and the role he'd
planned for me. I was determined to make a good impression, to
listen carefully, but the mesas distracted me. While he talked about
library architecture and paging and file system dumps, I wondered
what it must have been like to have ridden a horse into that desert,
with no idea of what was to come, to have seen those objects on the
horizon and felt a stirring of excitement and of fear, certain there
were no giants on the land and yet what were they, what else could
they be? The mesas were strange and marvelous to me but by
knowing there were such things, and even something about them,
I deprived myself of a certain drama, a full appreciation of the other,
the outside, the terrible and pristine. It occurred to me that adventure,
in the end, rises from ignorance; the less you know, the easier it is
to be a hero, and the more wonder there is to be found.

I looked up to find Willie both indulgent and annoyed as he
watched me. His oddly insubstantial fingers rested motionless in his
lap. I was embarrassed. Before he began again to speak, dryly, about
memory allocation and parallel processing, a look passed between

us, the only fully human contact I'd had, really, through two whole days of orientation and introduction and setting to my tasks. His message to me was that he understood my reservations, but that I had better either come in all the way or leave—no standing just by the door, coat in hand. Mine, to him, was that I needed the sky.

Willie was a respected figure at the company, widely considered to know more than anybody else about the software, a complex, convoluted mass of evolutions and accretions verging on the impenetrable. Born just a few years before me, he was an old hand, having started as a teenager with the operating system we were trying to produce yet another version of, staying with it over the years, working on one component or another, changing organizations from time to time and changing roles as well but always with his finger on its pulse, noting everything that was going on in the small but crowded universe that surrounded it. His grasp of history—a powerful asset when working on a product that was always being "developed" but was never done—was more detailed and reliable than anyone else's. If you wanted to know why something had happened a certain way, or what had become of this idea or that initiative, or whether anybody had ever tried what you wanted to try, you asked Willie. He seemed to have an aura, and the vigor of his movements, his large eyes and frail figure, his unruly hair like a boy's were almost flamboyant. It turned out (though I didn't learn it from him, and I don't think he would have told me) that he had invented and coded an old and basic function, known to every user. That made him a sort of celebrity, a frog of at least medium size in an idiosyncratic pond.

This was all what I gathered, not what I knew. Probationary as I was, unsure of my position, I worked hard to search out and piece together whatever indications I had access to, but I was always aware that they weren't enough. The circumstances were like no others I'd encountered, and I couldn't will them into making sense to me. Still, I was impatient; I had always had something to say about what

I experienced and survived, and as I could not bring myself to simply observe, to watch and wait, I was driven to appreciate and to define.

Therefore it surprised me, once I had grasped how important Willie was to the project, how greatly he was depended on, to realize that he was by no means in charge, that he had an undesirable office, that he worked long hours like the rest of us. It amazed me that I could hint at things I knew with great certainty to be true—I had gotten them from Willie, I was sure I had understood him correctly, and I had confirmed them through what I read and what I saw on the videotapes—and have the engineers chuckle, or take strenuous exception. It astounded me when the company's plans underwent sudden, radical alteration, when ongoing efforts were wrestled into a tight curve and sent off in some apparently random direction, all on the basis of a discovery or contingency that seemed both inconsequential and beside the point.

I learned to rely on keeping my mouth shut; on asking, when I opened it, the sort of broad, tired question—"What do I need to know about static processes, Sandra?"—that made me sound knowledgeable and bored but was really designed to tease out a bit of hard information on which I could build an understanding; and on my reference materials. I had been wise enough to buy, before I started, several indexed, concise guides to the system, avoiding the deeper texts. Had I tried to make my way through those, to follow my days in their pages, I would have gone under very quickly. Instead, while I groped for comprehension, I had instructions for the tools I needed to do my job—tools I'd led Cynthia, the woman who hired me, to believe I had used extensively in the past—and a basic and accessible (if often inadequate) definition of anything identified to me as that with which I should be familiar. All I had to do was bide my time until I could get back to my office and check my sources; it was precarious, but it worked. It got me through the beginning, the part that might otherwise have spooked me and made me run, despite all the reasons I had for staying put.

According to our arrangement, I split my time between my duties as Willie's scribe, sidekick, and audience-on-demand and my training with the technical writers, whom I was ultimately to join. They were less alien than the software developers and more my type than the marketing, financial, and legal contingents; most of them were, like me, refugees of one kind or another. Cynthia was (or had been) a Shakespeare scholar. Some of the others came from publishing, and several were ex-teachers. None had seen quite the joyride I'd put myself through—they were all accustomed to steady jobs and steady paychecks and appeared to be sensible, even sober, about the advantages of furthering their careers in computers, though not without dismay at the prospect, and thoughts of escape—but they all understood, unlike most others in the building, how narrow a slice of life our enterprise really was. Despite the casual dress and limited decorum of the engineers I was often anxious about my manner, my clothes, the topics I discussed in the cafeteria; I felt I didn't fit in and wasn't the right sort of person, that on such a basis I would be denied this opportunity to earn a comfortable living. I was saved from my distress by the technical writers, who made it clear that, as nonconformism was the standard of the software world, they chose not to be ostentatiously or even overtly nonconformist, but that despite this, in fact because of it, they were the true outsiders, and I was one of them. They liked me for my amiability and my talk about books and plays and traveling in Asia, and I liked them because they spared me some of my anxiety about what the job required of me. When someone whose eyebrow might be raised by our discussion joined us, they steered the conversation elsewhere or shut it down entirely, so deftly that many outside our circle never noticed we had one.

These people—and a couple of others, like the older secretary downstairs, whose husband ran the box office at the ballet and sent me tickets I'd never asked for—shared something with me. There were also those who were unknown, but appealing. I couldn't imagine how it was to be them, but I wanted them to consider me a friend.

Cynthia, like Willie, was a little odd-looking. She was tall, but the height was entirely in her legs. Her eyes were penetrating. Her hair was always wilder than it should have been, given her neat outfits and precise manner. Something about the tone of her skin was not quite right, and she appeared to have occasional brief lapses of consciousness. I wondered if she had lupus or some unusual anemia, one of those diseases I knew nothing about. That distressed me, and made it difficult for me to be at ease with her. Walking past her office, I often saw her staring out her window, hands poised on her keyboard, utterly still. I didn't know whether she was thinking about whatever she was typing, or watching the clouds go by, or simply resting, or in a trance. I wanted to go in, at some of these moments, and place my hands on her shoulders and my chin on her head; I wanted to push her off her chair; I wanted to give her something fresh and living to occupy that room with her, overfilled as it was with texts and piles of paper and black plastic binders, and souvenirs and citations marking a career I wanted to believe had only happened to her, as if she were an innocent bystander, rather than taking shape in her hands.

There was a great deal to do. I read the memos and project plans and outlines and reports and proposals and tutorials that were given me—I was genuinely astounded by the amount of paper that crossed my desk, it was of a volume such as I might barely have imagined for some solitary, obsessive, pained academic in an arcane and marginal discipline—and edited what the technical writers asked me to edit. I did my best to make Willie's thoughts, notes, explanations, and drafts into documents of my own. Though I was sometimes relaxed, I was frequently overwhelmed and panicky. Despite my preparations and plans, I often wondered—idly, but with feeling—how long it would be before I could allow myself to think of moving on.

It was very important at this stage of my life, as I had been told so emphatically by my former girlfriend and my parents and others, that I choose a project, any project, and finish it, see it through, "give it a real chance" at the very least, not because it would enrich or educate or substantiate me to do so but because I never had. I resented these opinions, but I knew the truth in them. I recognized the life I'd led as the product of my deep distrust of entitlement and obligation, rather than a genuine taste for a brief, serial existence. I was no dilettante; I admired those who plunged themselves in to the shoulder, who wrestled with the angel until long after their strength had given out, and most of what I valued in people was the product of sustained application, with no guarantee or even promise of reward.

There was so much I had to reject, so much that was lacking, such a saturating impermanence about my person and my past that to commit myself to anything had always implied a profound self-betrayal. I couldn't decide how it had started, which chicken had come from which egg, but each abandonment, each withdrawal, each surrender, had only deepened my futility, made it more difficult to contemplate the acceptance of any fate. Something was wrong, and I must wait for it to change itself; I must be ready for the world to fly apart and be reassembled in an instant. If my wandering, my dabbling, my distaste for the accumulation of substance and property had a motto, it was this: when the long and frightening night is over I will fill the day with my industry. Except the night did not end, and my childhood friends and classmates bought houses and had babies; a woman I genuinely loved left me because she could no longer defer her plans; my family and associates began to lose their respect for me; and as I saw that I was no longer admired I understood, at last, that I needed to be.

I had gathered, with difficulty and effort, a small stake, enough to get me a studio apartment and a few presentable items of clothing, and to allow me to accept Cynthia's offer of a temporary, low percentage of her minimum technical writing salary. It was a lifeline—far from the thickest, strongest one imaginable—and that was clear to her as well as to me. She was a friend of relatives and knew a little of my history, and I had been at pains to be open with her. I was, I let her know, someone who had never worked except for an hourly wage, who had never had benefits beyond worker's compensation and paid holidays, who had labored for a day to earn the night's shelter and would go back to that if he had to.

And while I exaggerated what I'd learned about computers during my two years at college—in particular my knowledge of the company's operating system—I was frank in saying that I wasn't sure her position was right for me, nor I for it. A canny person, concerned about the organization's welfare as a contributor to her own, she was inclined in any event to test me, and she didn't want me to "come on board" (a phrase I despised whenever I heard it, from the first time to the last) until I was sure it was what I really wanted. We made an agreement: she would pay me very little, by her standards, and I would "support" Willie for six months, until he made his presentation to the Operating Committee, at the same time becoming more familiar with the software, learning to be a technical writer, and doing odd jobs for the group. In the end we would meet and talk. If we both felt it was for the best, and if Willie and the writers approved, she would hire me as a permanent employee.

It irked me to be there on a trial basis, to be incompetent until proven competent, an outsider until ushered in, but it pleased me as well. I had become attached to a ghostly existence, to the leaving of no mark on the landscape over which I traveled, defying the voices of those who told me, time after time, that I could alter it in any way I chose. I had disappointed them into silence at last. This opportunity to start from nothing, to fairly prove myself—to this new world, after the old had all but given up—was a soothing prospect, almost joyful. Having scorned and squandered my early treasure, I badly wanted Cynthia and the others to approve of me, to praise me.

My beginnings at the company were not entirely smooth. Everyone thought well of me and saw me as intelligent and capable but there was as great deal I didn't know, a fact I tended to deny. Having spent so long annoying and impressing people I didn't respect by asking questions and learning everything long before they'd dreamed I could, I found myself, perversely, changing tactics at just the wrong time; with these, who would have appreciated an inquisitive approach, I was defensive and guarded instead.

On top of this it was difficult work; the writing was hard, the technical side was often excruciatingly dense, I had to take cogent, useful notes during long meetings of stupefying monotony. Above all, I was deflated by the ease with which my colleagues handled their duties. I took great pride in my writing skill and had been hoping to show that there was a place, even a need for me in this particular, self-absorbed world, but instead I found myself surrounded by any number of good writers and several who were excellent, and as I was realizing this I also discovered that my own abilities were untested, or at least rarified; they wilted and withered in the face of the mass of information I had to process, the short deadlines, the confusion generated in me by the videotapes and development group meetings and every second or third page I read. Rather than leading, I struggled to keep up; rather than writing fluidly, prolifically, as I had anticipated, I escaped for minutes at a time by playing games on my computer and chatting with my officemate, or by calling up the voice mail system and pressing "4" repeatedly, so I could hear the mechanical woman say "You have no messages" again and again.

I got much more satisfaction from my work with Willie. We seemed able to be productive, and mutually supportive. Along with the apparent clarity of his own thoughts, he had a knack for revealing what he knew, at least to me, a talent that made it difficult for me not to like him. He was always able to bypass preliminaries and quickly provide whatever I needed: missing information, an adjusted perspective, or a useful analogy through which I could grasp something previously opaque. I hated being lectured, and Willie had no need of it; he was brief and direct, and soon I was too.

We settled into a regular routine: I would see him in his office at mid-morning, review our recent progress with him, listen to him talk for a while and take notes if I needed to, and leave with a set of tasks to occupy me until we met again. Most of them had to do with creating and assembling a huge document—it was called a "specification," rather than a report or a plan—to be presented by Willie to the Operating Committee. If the committee liked it—that is, if they thought the efforts and goals it dictated were plausible, feasible, and desirable—it would define the company's software development policy for the next two years. (If they didn't like it, presumably Willie would be in disfavor or disgrace, though I didn't know what that would mean for him, or what they would base their plans on instead.) It was a very broad document, encompassing highly technical aspects of the machines and their instructions on the one hand and things like competitive advantage and corporate alliance on the other. It was eagerly awaited, and Willie and I were responsible for it; that made me interested and even excited. It soon became something I wanted to nurture, to cultivate.

The specification preoccupied us, but not at every moment, and I was cautious when we strayed from it. Willie seemed to want something from me; it distressed me that I didn't know what. Despite his peculiar mildness, his interest created a strain, almost a weight. The things on his walls suggested shared values but also inspired doubt, because I suspected their intent was not to establish his presence, or to tell who he was, but to elicit from us—from me—a confirmation of his person.

He was relentlessly inquisitive; he demanded to know what I

thought. But whereas the technical writers listened without asking, he asked and then appeared not to listen, or at least not to regard what I said as a description of me. He seemed inclined to talk about himself, but only if I provided an atmosphere, and boundaries, and even then what he revealed was more hidden than expressive.

"What's your opinion of all this?" he asked one day, as I was gathering my papers in the process of leaving his office.

"Of all what?" I said.

"Of your work here. Of the organization. Of the industry."

"How much do you want to know?"

He was briefly hesitant—as if reviewing our exchange for errors—and then smiled. "You must understand," he said, "that I never talk about this with anyone who isn't part of it. My wife and friends are all in it; I almost live in it. Sometimes I try to remember what it was like when I was a kid, before I was an odd person who knew strange things." He reached for his coffee mug and looked into it, then leaned back in his chair, crossing his legs. "There weren't very many of us, at first. It tended to cut me off. I guess it still does."

"You must see people who do other things," I said, holding my clipboard and folders in front of me. "Your neighbors, or the parents of your children's friends."

"But they know nothing about it and they don't want to discuss it. Except when a disk drive or printer needs fixing, and then I'm a technician." I glanced at a forest scene, at his daughter's portrait of the dog they didn't have. "They don't care," he said, without rancor. "But you do. I'm curious about your thoughts."

I put my materials on a corner of his desk. "It certainly is demanding," I said. "There's a lot to it. Sometimes I'm fascinated." I was conscious of sounding as if I wanted to flatter him. "I think a lot of time and work gets wasted, and there are things I could do without—the jargon and the meetings and all those stale jokes. And so much effort seems to go into aggrandizing everything. As if we had to be the most important people in the world."

Willie seemed attentive, if noncommittal. He sat very still, as he usually did, almost motionless. I noticed he'd been reading his messages; the characters on his screen glowed, and the cursor blinked steadily. "I suppose it's true," he said.

"Actually," I went on, "this is what amazes me: there are so many layers, and the people working on one level don't know what's happening on another. It's like a chemist who doesn't follow physics, or a biologist who doesn't know chemistry. You wonder how they can get anything done." I was speaking very quickly. "I see that nobody could keep up with all the information anyway, I know it's in the nature of the work, but everything is so disconnected. It's hard to understand."

Willie looked toward me, but not at me. I had come to expect these gaps in our conversations, to tolerate them, but this time I didn't like it. His walls were closing in, and I wanted to be back in my office, talking to the affable writer I shared it with. I reached for my clipboard.

"Sometimes I get overwhelmed," he said. "Sometimes I wonder if I haven't gotten a little crazy over the years."

I sat back, knowing he would go on, and now he did look at me—right at my eyes—and I felt, very strongly, as I often had, that he desired something from me, that he was on the verge of requiring what I was almost convinced I couldn't provide.

"My father was an auto mechanic," he told me. "He used to bring old parts home for us to play with. I think maybe I became an engineer because of him. He had all sorts of ideas for inventions and improvements, but he didn't have the training or education or time to do anything with them." He spoke as if repeating what he'd long ago lost interest in, but also as a man searching for something too important to have casually misplaced, looking one more time where he'd looked before because there was nowhere else he could possibly have put such a thing.

"Actually, he was too dumb," he went on. "Too dumb and happy. He made a pretense of being interested—he loved to talk—but he didn't really want anything to change."

"It's not so awful to be happy," I said.

"There's so much I don't understand," he said. "I work so hard, and they tell me I succeed, but I don't know where the results go." He gestured around him, a wave of the hand that was meant to encompass the two of us, or his brightly decorated cell, or the company, or our lives. "Thin air," he said.

Later that day, I was walking past an entrance to the machine room, where the large, powerful computers—the ones that connected the small workstations on our desks, so we could exchange mail and share information—were kept. I had never been inside; I didn't know the combinations of the large, gleaming pushbutton locks.

As I neared the door, it opened and one of the operators came out, then turned as if she'd forgotten something. I was seized with the desire to see for myself, to approach the center of the network. I wanted to physically touch the device. When she emerged again I moved purposely forward with my papers and clipboard, as if briskly on an errand, and grabbed the door at the extreme of its swing. She hardly knew I was passing.

I looked around me. The computers were evenly spaced along the perimeter of the room, five or six of them, varied in color and exact dimension but all essentially the same: featureless plastic boxes, not quite my height, with a few labeled buttons and lights on their fronts and smaller machines surrounding them. Each had tape readers and disk drives and too many cables to sort with my eyes, and each was connected to a nearby terminal, for maintenance and system commands.

Nothing was moving. There was a strange, interrupted quality to the room, an echo or a quiver, a continuous settling, as if someone had been working there for years, and gone away for a moment, and stayed away forever. My ears were filled with the powerful rush of the air conditioning as it fought endlessly against the heat of the machines, and the floor and walls were a clean, even off-white. Despite the sense of ongoing tension, I found it a comforting place. I stood, watching, no longer very curious but instead content, as if it would have pleased me to move my desk there, or my lunch hours, or even my own bed.

After some weeks at the company, I began to think I might last. They were weeks that rolled smoothly, gathering easily into months because their regularity, their structure—the abrupt beginning, the stretch through midweek that promised so much, the compression as I sensed the end and so furiously resented the meetings and the chores and the other time-wasters, the weekend during which I tried (despite myself, but like anyone else) to forget what I had just spent five days struggling to comprehend—was so compelling. It was like a square dance, or someone with a bullhorn commanding a crowd; the easiest thing was to go along.

Before coming to the company, I had always been either on or off, my weeknights merely shorter versions of the weekend, just as good for getting drunk, but this job claimed more from me than my presence and outer attention during certain hours of certain days. I needed to be, it seemed, a whole person when working, one who shared a great deal of what I had always been but was not entirely familiar. I found that I could no longer switch gears so smoothly, could not make the change merely by putting on my coat and going home. The simple rule was that my guise reflected the day of the week—was I in my sixty-four hours, or their one hundred and four?—but it wasn't always simple, nor was it entirely fair. The company wanted something from me that I did not ask in return;

while I was, for much of the week, on their clock, they were never on mine.

At times my interest in what the others thought of my work was formulaic, even abstract, and my own satisfaction seemed to be enough. On occasion I craved reassurance. As I thought about it, worried about it, questioned myself, I came to believe that Willie's evaluation would have the greatest weight, though he never showed he knew it. His personal demands, whatever their source, had no reference to the fact that he sat in judgment on me; along with Cynthia and the others he was always supportive, and apparently confident of my success.

No one ever suggested I might fail, but I heard a warning from somewhere. It nudged me, annoyed me, insinuated itself at incongruous moments, not when I was thinking the situation over, or sitting by the river staring at the oily, sluggish water, but as I shopped for groceries, or called a movie theater to check the times. It came forcefully to my dreams, in perplexing forms—like the chair with a demon embedded in its seat, a furry-faced demon whose rapid speech was bizarre, though not entirely threatening, and very intent—and in scenes that should have been pleasant or mundane but filled me with a sort of nervous dissatisfaction, a conviction that I'd been somehow cheated or deprived. I resolved to be patient, but it was hard; I honestly didn't know what I hoped for, and it slowly became clear that their encouragement interfered as much as it helped. I was called on, not unfairly, to state clearly yes or no, and I needed to consider in peace, left alone with my fancies and my humors.

The likelihood of my getting a permanent position made the question of permanent associations—the co-worker as friend—more pressing. My inclination from the beginning had been to confine relationships to the building itself, and to relatively impersonal interaction. I managed this mostly by controlling conversation very strictly. It was one thing to go on about Sherwood Anderson over hamburgers and fries, but those who pressed me for details about myself, or pursued discussion when I wasn't so inclined, learned that I was willing to draw very firm lines. I was surprised that no one challenged my aloofness, but it suited me; I was in the habit of holding myself apart, and the further we got from the work, the more likely they would be to see the fragments of my former lives.

It was common within the group to stage small gatherings for a variety of reasons: arrivals, departures, birthdays, maternity or paternity impending or in fact, deadlines met, projects completed, or Cynthia's feeling that we'd all been working hard and needed a party or maybe something good to eat, and not at our own expense. I avoided these gatherings at first but felt increasingly awkward about begging out of them. I disliked the thought of offending the other writers—though I wanted to, I could not explain that it was not them but myself I was keeping at a distance—so I gradually got in the habit of at least dropping by. I would not join them for the pale celebratory lunches at overpriced neighborhood restaurants, and it must have been clear that I wasn't enthusiastic about Wednesday afternoon bagels and fruit, but I handed over my dollar bills and signed the cards and generally contributed an appearance and a few words of conversation.

Around four o'clock one day, Cynthia stopped by to invite me and my office-mate to a party at her house, on the weekend. I had plans, not yet definite, to spend that evening at a movie, and in any case my reflexive impulse was to say no—because it was entirely unexpected and for some reason alarming—but the two of them seemed determined to expose me, looking silently at me as if prompting my answer, as if they had arranged beforehand that they would wait for me to speak. It appeared to matter in some new way. When I told her, a little stiffly, that it sounded like fun, the moment was finished and she withdrew.

Later, going home on the subway, I found myself filled with questions about my fellow travelers—the tired, edgy office workers, the teenagers I had lately felt so removed from, the older riders both disconcerted by and resigned to their transformed surroundings, the men in dirty clothes and worn-out shoes, homeless or laborers or both—and about their hopes, their expectations, the things they settled for. Most were dissatisfied, surely, but were they content with their dissatisfaction? Did they accept it, like lost solitude or pain from a loved one? Was it something they would miss if it were gone?

On Saturday I made myself a large dinner and didn't eat it. I waited, watching TV shows I didn't want to watch, because it seemed important to be a late arrival at the party; I tried to laugh when I found myself discarding, in a panic, the first outfit I'd put on. I understood that I was struggling to choose between the well-defined but fragile company man I had so recently dreamed up and the me I had always taken to parties, knowing as I compared them that a third, more daring soul was watching, waiting to throw his weight one way or the other, or (surely) to strike out on his own. The realization of just how uncertain I was almost kept me in my room but I conjured the prospect of a sort of reversion, a suspension of my probation, of going to Cynthia's as if the guests would be old, tolerant friends and I could entirely disregard the effect of what I said or did in front of them. That was enough to set me on my way.

I'd believed, smugly, before she invited me, that Cynthia and her husband had a house in the suburbs. Surprised by the city address in the photocopied directions she'd given me, I discovered that it was in a sophisticated and trendy district, in fact in the very heart of the action. On a rainy evening, in the warm weather, their neighborhood acted on me like movies and songs and clever advertisements, made me want to belong. And when Cynthia opened the door of her apartment, I saw that it was large and attractive, and filled with interesting objects, some of genuine beauty. There were paintings and small sculptures and books I wanted, and furniture, and the guests were not the homogeneous, narrow collection of middle-class industry types I'd expected; they were flamboyant and stylish, of widely varied background and age and ethnicity, and they were chattering busily, almost wildly, to each other. Few were from the company, as far as I could tell, and I was disconcerted to find that several of the technical writers I'd expected had stayed away, or had come and gone, or had not yet arrived.

Rudy was Cynthia's husband. Short and chubby, partly Italian— he'd arrived with his parents as a boy, he said as he gestured around with the drink he was getting me, pointing out the friends he'd made in a local immigrants' aid organization—he was warm, well spoken and humorous. His courtesy made me graceless, and his unstudied appearance made me feel overdressed, but he so clearly welcomed me that I was immediately his friend. I thought at first that Rudy and Cynthia were an odd couple, but when I saw them together—rushing around the kitchen, or greeting guests just inside the door—they appeared to be very well matched.

Willie's presence was perhaps the biggest surprise of all, though it shouldn't have been. He and Cynthia were old friends, but I'd forgotten it, or ignored it; in any case I hadn't expected to find him there and I hadn't wanted to, and when I saw him standing in a corner, waving at me, I was brought to ground. The scene around me, growing more kaleidoscopic and indefinite and chaotic and exciting every moment, was suddenly resolved into sharp-edged, cool, manageable reality by the sight of him. I turned away, quickly, but as I did I waved back—I couldn't help myself—and he started toward me. I looked for the couple I'd been talking to, but they were gone.

"Where's your wife?" I asked him as he neared.

"At home with sick children," he said. He looked me up and down. "And is this the real you?"

It was so shallow, so conventionally unfunny, that it annoyed me.

I felt justified in my irritation, no matter his intent. Though he, like me, was as he'd always been, he seemed now an eager hunter, roaming in search of a prize. I smiled and sipped my drink.

"What about you?" he asked. "Are you here with someone?" I shook my head. As I did, a woman I'd noticed—you couldn't help but notice her—caught my eye again. She was lovely, but she might not have been; there was nothing about her (except maybe the color of her skin, a brown that made me think of dry hills and oriental rivers, or of a horse in a bright field of grass, in the morning) that was overwhelmingly beautiful or remarkable. Her appeal, I'd observed, was not of fixed location; at times I thought it must reside in me, not in her, as if I had prior cause for wanting her, as if I already had for years, from afar.

Willie followed my eyes. "You must be glad you came alone," he said, "or sorry. I will say she looks just right for you."

Through the evening it went on that way: wherever I went, Willie would find me eventually, and he would comment on me as if he'd been asked to, like an intern expounding on a patient's vital signs, or as if I were two people, the one he was talking to and the one he was talking about. But I was reluctant to force him away. Had he spoken falsely or insulted me I might have been angry, but I couldn't accuse him of that, and the substance of much of what he said or hinted at—I was fascinated despite myself—diminished, though it shouldn't have, the offense I felt at the intrusion. His crime was mostly speaking rightly at the wrong moment, and persistently so; no sooner had I set a new blind then he would flush me out of it.

When he wasn't examining me he told me stories, tales of his childhood and adolescence. Several were morbid, like the one about his best friend who died skiing, because of a mismarked trail, just before his twenty-first birthday. As always, he was greatly in earnest, and seemed to think that my comments, my answers, were the only function of our interaction. In a room full of people he kept coming back to me.

It was confusing and upsetting, being chased by Willie around and through a party I was trying to crash but couldn't quite get at, as if all these jolly, colorful, quick people were behind plate glass, or hired actors who felt called on by their parts to acknowledge my presence and speak to me on current events but weren't really interested at all. There were glimpses throughout of the woman who made me yearn so—never alone, never approachable—and of Cynthia and Rudy, whom I found I so fiercely admired that only politeness kept me from doing my best to monopolize their attention, politeness and the certainty that as soon as I'd managed to attract it my tagalong, Willie, would be there to take it from me.

By twenty past eleven I'd had too much to eat, and to drink; I felt bloated and slow. I was exhausted from dodging Willie, and from the strain of hiding resentment and dismay. I was ready to stop running away from him, to stop trying to attach myself to guests who looked especially interesting, to abandon any thought of approaching the brown-skinned woman. He found me again as I sat on the couch, across from the kitchen door, eyeing the chocolate cake on the coffee table.

"I'll start it if you're afraid to," he said, almost gently.

"Willie, I am not afraid to cut into a cake," I said. "It's only a cake." I leaned over the table. "If I'm afraid of anything I'm afraid of being fat, but as it happens I'm beyond caring."

"I used to worry about being fat," said Willie as he watched me cut a piece.

"You? You're like a rail."

"I used to be concerned about any number of things that don't matter now," he said. "I've changed a great deal."

The cake was wonderful. I hadn't had chocolate cake like it in a long time; it evoked early childhood, a pure and ancient pleasure.

It was so good that I ate very slowly, wanting to wake up and remember it the next morning.

"I see that I don't have a sense of myself," Willie was saying. "I've lost that whole aspect." There was a vagueness to his address; I thought, with satisfaction, that he was finally running down. "I don't know what to value," he said.

And there she was, standing nearby, looking the table over to see if there was anything she wanted. Willie kept talking and I wished intensely that he would shut up, and that I didn't have chocolate cake on my lap and at the corners of my mouth, and that I could use my napkin without calling her attention to the fact that I needed to. Our eyes met as I looked at her; it was exciting to see that she was flustered by my glance, and not displeased.

She seemed on the verge of speech, but was distracted by Willie. "I'm not a very interesting man," he said to me. "I've chosen that, I know, but it still hurts to find it's true." Cake in my mouth, eyes on this beauty, I was nonetheless aware that there was a disturbance in his voice, a purpose I hadn't heard before. "I admire you," he said. I was ashamed. I wanted to hurt him to make him stop; I wanted to grip his wrist and squeeze until he thought the bones would crack.

Amused, disconcerted, she turned away, as if to walk on. I cleared my mouth frantically.

"It's good," I said. She turned back. "The cake. It's fabulous."

She brightened immediately. "Is it?" she asked.

"*He* thinks so," said Willie, gesturing at the sloppy crumbs on my lap.

I can't say what she thought of that; I'm not even sure what I would have said. I don't know what might have happened had Cynthia not come out of the kitchen, just then, and asked me to go and get some ice. I was a second late, at most, in grasping that all I had to do was suggest to the woman that she join me; she drifted away as Willie volunteered to go along, and as Cynthia asked for beer as well.

After the noise of the party, the streets were calm and empty. The wet surfaces shone. The fresh air helped us both, I think; we walked down the sidewalk quickly, without speaking. A minute before I had wished him gone, but now I was calming and I appreciated his silence; he was allowing me, at last, to withhold myself. Perhaps he understood. When we got back to the party he would let me be.

I almost wanted—thinking of those misty crags in Willie's office, ominous and strong—to reach out and take his hand as he walked beside me. Strangely, I felt that everything could be fine and could work out for the best, that the gleaming streets and passing cars and the facades of the apartment buildings, windows lit or dark at random, were protecting and supporting us, guaranteeing us favorable winds.

We found the liquor store as Cynthia had described it, and it did have ice, as well as the beer we were after. It was a cluttered place, with more neon than stores twice its size, and shelves of every depth and height to hold a huge variety of bottles. The plastic structure that framed the woman who sat behind the counter was so covered with merchandise and printed matter that it resembled an overgrown arbor; festooned with toys and little signs, packages of nuts and chips, lottery tickets and pens, cigarette lighters and rolling papers, souvenir key chains and postcards, it was both festive and historical, almost eloquent. To venture into this place and come out again, under the streetlights, with simple supplies—the six-packs under Willie's arms and the bag of ice cradled in my hands—was like a short journey to a kingdom, to some magical den, to purchase potions and charms, only to find when we emerged that the gold was lead again, and the talking flower was still.

I turned to Willie to make some remark about the store. I didn't expect him to be glaring at me the way he was, partly in anger, partly wounded and bitter.

"You don't approve of me, do you?" he asked.

For an instant it seemed only absurd, but unprepared as I was for the question I found I had an answer—or at least a response—all ready for him. "Why does it matter so much if I do?" I said. "What is it you want from me?" I looked back at him, briefly but directly. "From me, of all people?" We started walking. It had been just three or four minutes from Cynthia's house to the store; whatever exchanges were to be made would have to be made quickly. Willie had his head down, and I thought he might be smiling, but I would have had to stop to find out.

"Look, Willie," I said, "I like you. I'm very forthcoming but I won't be forced. You suggest that I owe something. You make me feel—pursued." This silence—I was sure he'd answer, but he just kept walking, and so did I—was unlike the other, but it built on what that had suggested. For better or worse, I knew we were intimate now, close, even touching in a way I'd successfully resisted until this moment, not because he'd finally provoked me into stridency, into rudeness, but because I hadn't laughed, I hadn't dismissed him, I hadn't told him to get lost, in effect, as I could easily have done. When we arrived at Cynthia's building I turned to face him.

"Willie, what do you think I know?" I asked him. "What do you see in me? Is there something I said? Something I've forgotten?"

He carefully placed the six-packs at my feet. "What makes you so different?" he asked. "What makes you so far apart?" Then he walked away. I stood and watched him go, though the ice was by now very cold in my hands. A few yards distant, he turned to face me and started to speak, then caught himself, and somehow—with his gesture and his face, and what he might have told me—expressed despair. "Oh, who do you think you are?" he said at last, and was gone.

As I went around that block, and then another, the beer under

the stairs in Cynthia's lobby and the ice melting on the stoop, I
thought about what he might mean to me, why he disturbed me so.
How could I ask him what I couldn't answer? I came, as I had
many times before, to the passion I should have shown him instead
of the helpless shrug he got.

"You're a jerk, Willie," I said aloud. "I'm a lousy choice."

I turned, to be sure he wasn't following me. "I don't know how
this *happened*," I said. I actually did a little stamping dance on the
sidewalk, I was so baffled, so frustrated. I kicked a brick wall. "I
don't see any point!"

Raising my eyes, knowing somehow, I saw a boy, with his arms
on the windowsill and his head on his arms, watching and listening.
In my drama, I was his small parade. Our eyes met. I was glad to
be beyond any need to disarm him, or to explain, but I was disappointed that I couldn't speak, sorry for what I couldn't say; he waited
so patiently.


It was two weeks later that Willie left the company. He was there
one day and gone the next; he'd emptied his office literally overnight,
and I went to stand and look at the spot where the mesas had been.

In the days between the party and his departure, Willie and I
had worked amiably together. Of course everything was changed,
but I had resolved to salvage as much as I could. I couldn't act as
if nothing had happened, but I wanted to state that what we'd been
through did not require us to be other than what we already were.
My manner towards him at first reminded me—it made me smile—
of a phone call I'd made to my girlfriend, the day after the first
night we spent together, to tell her that no one was going anywhere,
that there was plenty of time to take it in, that we would have the
chance to discuss everything. I'd assumed he felt the same way. If
he was in distress there was no trace of it, not by the end of our
first morning meeting, an hour we spent talking about work amid

the familiar drawings and photographs, under the ceiling grill that I no longer watched so carefully.

It was rumored that he'd resigned because there was too much in the specification that wasn't as he thought it should be—an incredible assertion to me, because I believed I would certainly have been the first to know it if he felt that way—and because its rejection by the Operating Committee was all but certain. This new information about our project should have pleased me, confirming my ability to keep at arm's length what I would rather not know, but it made me angry. I wanted to argue. I wanted to defend our work, but I knew if I did I would make myself a fool.

It was also said that he had some kind of serious personal problem, a disturbance that the gossipers loved to hint at but would not detail. Cynthia and the few others who considered themselves his friends went through the halls tight-lipped and skittish; I was tempted to believe that they knew the whole story and refused, out of loyalty and regard, to tell it, but that may have been wishful thinking, a desire to impart a nobility to the episode, a decency it should have had but lacked. The one time I almost asked Cynthia—she was notorious for her ability to keep a secret, and I had no doubt about which of us mattered most to her, but I thought perhaps she would understand that I needed to gauge my own blame—I remembered her look when I returned to her apartment, with beer and a bag of ice water and no Willie, and immediately gave it up.

There was only so much wondering I could do. That Willie had been able to handle himself with dignity, to resist piling worse upon bad and requiring us to offend each other further, made it all the more telling, and painful, that he'd withdrawn from me—cut everyone off—so definitely and completely. But however I'd figured in Willie's decision, whatever my effect on the orbit of his life, I found it didn't concern me. My eyes were on myself.

Leaving—backing out, signing off, resigning, refusing, or just disappearing in the dead of night—was nothing new to me. I was

sure it would have given many of my colleagues a degree of satisfaction to quit with some dramatic gesture, a grand rejection of the
company's world and the nations of employees within it, but I had
been through that before. I had deprived myself of too much by
behaving as if nothing mattered; stay or go, swim or sink, I intended
to treat my circumstances with respect. A departure like Willie's,
without explanation but with enough probable cause that we were
left to guess and be half right, distorted everything; somehow, though
he'd made his own choices, he'd been abused, or deprived. It was
an ugly reality. To beg the question of what went wrong—by throwing the job in the company's face, or by sneaking away without
words—was to deny that we did this work for reasons, to pretend
that it was not the substance of our lives, and to reject, ultimately,
our own significance.

I was returning to my office one day from a meeting with an
editor, thinking about Willie, when I decided to stop at the kitch-
enette and see if there was any decaffeinated coffee. There wasn't,
and as I made it fresh I was uplifted by the process: scrubbing out
the pot with the orange spout, rinsing the basket, separating a clean
white filter from the stack, tearing the green plastic pouch perfectly,
without spilling a single grain, leaving an opening of a size and
shape that let me pour the coffee out smoothly and with confidence.
I felt great affection for the equipment, and the magazines scattered
on the table, and the sun through the window, and the late afternoon
quiet around me. Even as it came to me it seemed a little silly, but
I felt for the first time entirely in place, that without question I could
belong there. I also understood, with sadness and finality, that though
it accepted my contribution, the company had nothing to do with
me; my frustrations, my convictions mattered to it not at all; we
would pass, again and again, but never meet, and some day it would
not even remember my name.

Carrying my cup in one hand and my folders in the other, I went
to Cynthia's office to find her at her desk, hands motionless over

the keyboard, gazing down to her side, at the floor. I knocked; as she saw me I walked in, and sat in the corner.

"Cynthia, I don't think I'm going to take the job," I said.

At times Cynthia was as changeable and expressive as a child; at others she was impassive, even stony. Had she shown disappointment, frustration, or anger I would have squirmed, but I would have welcomed it. For a moment I believed she would sit there forever, not speaking, just looking at me.

"I haven't offered it to you yet," she said.

"I felt you were going to."

"I was going to," she said. Immediately, something shifted; my decision became real. We sat comfortably together, if not as friends then as comrades of long-ago.

"That's a lot of work you put in for nothing." She looked at me. We heard some people in the corridor, talking and laughing; then they were gone. "I'm wrong," she said.

"Not for nothing," I said.

"Does this have anything to do with Willie?" she asked.

I started to tell her yes; I started to tell her no; I understood that there was now a great deal she could say, was prepared and even eager to say, about Willie, about herself, about me. It was a talk I didn't want to have, but it was important to be courteous, even tender; she had lost something too. In the end the best I could do was to shrug and smile, and to offer my hand.

There were tasks for me to finish, a string of hours to be worked out, arrangements to be made for my final payment, even (if I stood still for it) a farewell lunch, or at least a party with cake and ice cream, but that afternoon, as I walked home—a forty-minute trip I'd taken just a few times before—I felt movement, direction, a sureness I hadn't known for years, perhaps not ever. To be so much at loose ends, with no job or savings or plans, and yet so thoroughly without concern was peculiar, and very satisfying. To be not content or disappointed, but merely to be: that, for once, was enough. I surveyed with admiration the people that surrounded me; they were my fellows, my companions. They were my ideal.

It was not that I was giving up, nor was I concluding that I had been wrong to try. It was entirely a matter of deciding—or of discovering, shyly but definitely, with the clarity, the grace that comes over you all of a sudden, like the light of home—that as it was I who must determine what would make me happy, then I also must choose what would make me real.

To have an effect, to be a presence on the face of the earth, you must defend the place you occupy and reject the one that is given you; you must struggle to remain who you are. To be other than a wraith, an impression, a memory, you must dispute and pursue, you must give in to passion, you must want and be denied. I had arrived at the center of my own attention; what was missing, all along, was me. I sat on my bench by the river, that filthy, unadorned, unappreciated band of water that had flowed past long before I ever laid eyes on it, and wondered that I had wasted so much of my time.

People tell me that they live in houses for years, even decades, and then move away, leaving them miles behind, to find that they never think of them, that their new homes become the place they have always been. Leaving the company was like that for me; after a lifetime of rejecting the idea of loss, of refusing to gain that which I might not be able to hold, I amazed myself. I was able to walk away with an utter lack of regret.

One piece that I wanted was missing. Willie and I had business undone. He had touched me in my isolation; I felt he hadn't understood me, hadn't known me, and I wanted him to. Although I had sensed from the beginning his requirements, his strange urgency, it was he, in the end, who had not asked me to turn inside out, to stand on my head, to become something for his sake as if it were for mine.

And it disappointed me, the prospect of losing track of him. If my days at the company were to become, over time, a confused, inchoate dream, he was still the nut, the kernel of it; his face stood out with a clarity nothing else shared. Willie was my memento. I wanted to know what happened to him, whether he changed anything, or rearranged his relationships—to the code, to the world, to himself—but I came to understand that even if he did, I would not be there to see it. I was able to accept the reality of knowing, of taking comfort in knowing, that he would fight his battles, as I would fight mine.

# · Ohio, 1931

"THIS is a picture of your father," she said. "Please, have more coffee."

He took the small, tarnished frame she handed him and looked silently at the image in it for nearly a minute. "I'm very happy to see this," he said. "I haven't ever seen one quite like this."

"It's yours," she said. "I want you to take it with you."

He looked at her, then at the photograph, then at her again. She was settled in her armchair, her feet on a small footstool he remembered, fondly, from childhood; she seemed glad he'd come. They were almost facing each other and almost side-by-side, because she'd asked him to move the chairs so they would be out of the sun but not too far from the window and the breeze, and still have somewhere to put their cups and saucers.

"Look on the back," she said.

She had described the scene on a piece of notepaper—from the Anderson Hotel, he noticed—and cut it to fit in the frame, behind the photograph. " 'Joey at the Zoo, on his sixth birthday, in Cincinnati,' " he read out loud. " 'The little girl is Sallie Levine, Sam Levine's younger sister. Joe and Sam used to hide from Sallie in the bushes behind my house on Polk Street.' "

"He gave me that for the Fourth of July," she said. "He bought that frame himself, from his allowance."

"I really couldn't take it from you," he said.

She shook her head. "Please don't argue with me," she told him. "When I heard you were coming I thought of it right away, and decided to pass it on to you. I thought you'd be glad to have it."

"I am, very much," he said. "I can't tell you how pleased I am." He looked at the picture again. A boy in shorts, a plain shirt, white socks and sturdy shoes was standing on a graveled path, looking over his shoulder at someone invisible behind him, pointing with emphasis to something ahead. The face from the portraits he already owned—two of a young man, one of a teenager, one of an infant, one of the father of three small children—was easy to recognize. Next to the boy was a little girl in a fancy white dress, her hands clasped in front of her, staring at whatever he was pointing to.

"But it must be important to you," he said. "I don't see how I can take it."

"It doesn't matter," she said. "I assure you it doesn't." He understood suddenly that she was giving things away because she felt she might die soon. She seemed embarrassed, and because he admired both her courage—she was ninety-one—and her generosity, he wanted to tell her not to be. But as she poured his coffee into the elegant blue cup before him, he knew she was embarrassed because he had made her explain it to him.

"I'm touched and grateful that you thought of me," he told her, trying very hard to say the right thing. "I'll think of you and my father whenever I look at it."

"And the wonderful times we had together," she said, smiling. "He was a wonderful, wonderful boy. He was terribly good to me."

"I've never been to Cincinnati," he told her. "Before I leave, I'd like it very much if you'd tell me about some of the places to look for when I finally do go."

"I'm sure I don't know what's worth seeing now," she answered. "It's been nearly thirty years since I lived there."

"Not as a tourist," he said. "I mean the house he grew up in, and your house, and the parks he played in. And his schools. Anything you remember."

She touched his knee, briefly. "I'm afraid most of it's gone, dear," she said. Her hand was very old but he could see the strength in it. "I'll tell you what I can."

He sipped and looked around the room. "It's lovely here," he said. Though she had more reason than most, he felt, to be demanding or dissatisfied—great age and the ills and pains that went with it, friends and family lost, unpleasant changes in the world around her, mounting up, year after year—she made him feel more welcome, more valued, than anyone he could think of. He'd arrived rumpled and greasy from the road; greeting him, exclaiming over him, she'd insisted he shower and rest. Later, waking him through the door, she'd promised fresh coffee. He'd dressed for her in the only clean clothes he had. He wished he was staying for a week, or more.

"I was so lucky to get this house," she said. "I've had nothing bad to say about it, in all this time." He looked through the window, at the lawn and the oak tree and a piece of the road beyond. "After supper," she said, "when it's cooler, we'll sit on the porch. I do that frequently in the warm weather."

He smiled at her, and she smiled back. "Is there anything I can do for you while I'm here, Aunt Jennie?" he asked. "Anything I can move or fix?" She shook her head, paused, shook her head again.

"Speaking of lovely," she said, "where's that girl of yours?"

"Gone," he said. He saw how it distressed her; he had spoken freely, forgetting himself. She was very adaptable, but she'd finished high school before the war with the Hun was over, before there were radios. He couldn't expect her to understand the way he lived his life. "We decided to take a vacation from each other," he explained. "We both feel we need time to think. She's with her family. She'll probably join me in Seattle."

"She'll probably join you?"

"She may join me," he said. "I'm sorry to tell you this—I know you liked her very much, and she liked you—but she may not come to Seattle. That is, we may not stay together."

She nodded her head. "I see," she said. "I'm saddened to hear it." She shifted in her chair, just a bit, slowly pushing on one armrest and inching herself over to one side. "Didn't you tell me in New York that you intended to marry her?"

"I may have," he said. "It's the kind of thing I say. And it was true, as far as it went."

"I would think she would be very pleased to marry you," she said. "I would think you would have only to ask her."

"That was probably so at one time," he told her. "I think I must have waited too long."

She leaned her head back against the chair, and closed her eyes. "I'm very sorry, David," she said.

"I know you are," he said. "Thank you."

She opened her eyes, briefly, then closed them again. Down the street he could hear children shouting, and a dog barking wildly, and he felt very strongly that she was sitting, silently, not watching him, so he could examine her, see her as she was—someone who'd been alone for the larger portion of her life—and consider that he might not want to subject himself to the same denials, the same constraints. The sun had shifted; shining through her thin hair, it made her very frail.

"I wish I had something to tell you that would help you to understand your father," she said, her eyes still closed. "I've wished that all these years. I didn't think it was my place to say anything, but I wanted to be ready, in case you asked."

"I've never asked," he said. "I don't think I ever asked anyone, not once. I guess I needed to believe that the grown-ups understood."

"Then you did well to avoid asking me," she said. "It would have been obvious to you that I had no idea at all. At least none I could put into words."

He sipped at his coffee. The cup he was drinking from, the figurine on the end table, the embroidered footstool, the glass-fronted cabinet filled with books and carvings and jewelry and clocks, were all so familiar to him that he wondered how many visits he had made to this house as a child. He'd remembered two, but now he knew it must have been more. He wondered briefly if he could picture her old house, that his father had played in and had sometimes slept in, but she'd left there when he was very small.

"I'm still not much help," she went on, "but I can tell you this: your father was the sweetest little boy in the world, and he loved me very, very much. For all the people I've known, I still get the warmest feeling I could have, remembering how we were together and how good he was to me. He couldn't have been more devoted if I was his real mother."

She opened her eyes and lifted her head, to look at him. It was as if she had energy only for that; the rest of her was relaxed and still. "I know," he said.

"You don't," she said. "You weren't there." Seeing his face, she lowered her eyes. "What I'm trying to say is that he did so many hurtful things later on—I know I can speak freely with you—but he was nothing but good to me. He never caused me any pain. He was a joy."

She was almost defiant.

"I'll be okay, Aunt Jennie," he said. Her hand began to tremble and he reached over and took it, more for lack of anything else that would ease her distress than because he felt close to her, although he did. He wanted to tell her that he would be sorry when she was gone, that he would be that much more alone, but he guessed, as she gripped his hand more tightly than he would have thought her capable of, that this was what she feared.

The next evening, in his motel room near Wichita, deciding to call Sarah, deciding against it—picking up the phone and putting it down and picking it up again, even dialing the first digit, then another, as if each progressive physical step would bring him that much closer to her without revealing him, so that he could feel, by the tension of his proximity, more exactly what he wanted to do about it all—he got out the photograph and studied it, wishing his father wasn't turned so much away, was looking right at him, wishing there were questions he could ask. He took the frame apart to search for notes on the back, or something about the paper that would yield a clue, but in handling it managed only to worry loose a piece of the emulsion, making a blank spot near his father's head, a hole in the surface, a permanent obstacle to the conviction that the photograph could, somehow, if he knew enough, provide for him, or give him back a moment of his precious time.

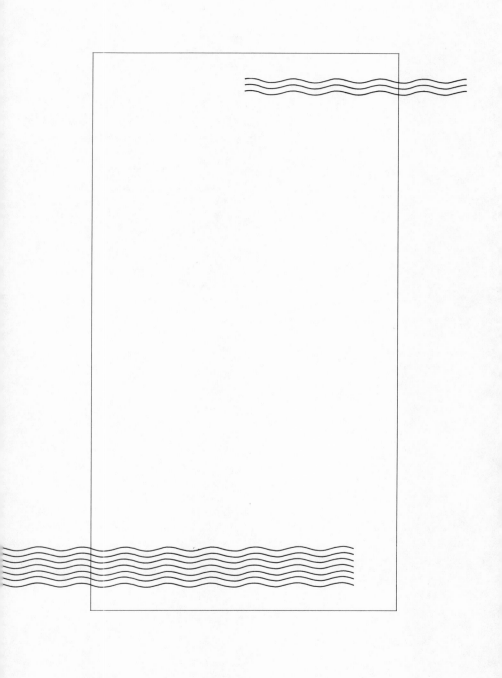

# · Calling
# Montgomery

HE always reassured her, even when the news wasn't good. His voice had that quality, as if his function were not to provide information, but to remind her that what he had to say was not as important as it might sometimes seem. The pleasure and excitement he found in giving his knowledge to her—she imagined him working through the night, a mug of coffee constantly in his hand, going over reports, checking and rechecking his instruments, rising from his desk to consult a reference—was distinct from the consequences he knew his words would have. The bottom line was one thing, the method by which he calculated it another.

If she called too late he was gone for the day; his replacement was as steady, occasionally as comforting, but the enthusiasm was missing. Montgomery was the leader, beginning the journey, relying on the others to hold to its course. She was almost certain that he was in charge, that Dave and the rest took their orders from him. All he asked, she knew, was that they respect what they were doing; his own involvement, his passion, was not something he could require.

Sensationalism was the fashion, and other sources were entirely unreliable. A chance of snow became the threat of a blizzard to rival memory's worst; high winds were always a hurricane, barreling up the coastline to transform the landscape and bring suffering and grief. Facts were important to her and she resented being toyed with. At the same time, she deeply disliked the aggrandizement of the mundane, though she understood the broadly shared concern. Everyone took the weather personally; it was always an appropriate topic, often the only agreeable one. She wished, though, that people would restrict that sort of thing to sports or movies or unsolved crimes, matters which were, in fact, trivial, and mostly made up of what was said about them. The temperature and the rain and snow were real, they caused distress and deprivation, they were much more powerful than most people wanted to acknowledge. They demanded respect.

Montgomery preferred not to upset anyone. He was never confident unless he was certain. If he could give probabilities, or even possibilities, he would; if not, he admitted he didn't know. He usually found a way, when he was through with the detailed forecast, to convey the overall mechanics of the situation in a brief but coherent statement, like a fortune from a cookie. She appreciated this. It was true that you had to be informed about the circumstances to follow him closely. You had to know that the area was a dumping ground for the continent, for the entire quadrant of the globe, with weather streaming up the coast from the islands and the gulf, down from the tundra, and across the miles of earth and forest from the mountains and the plains. You had to be familiar with the fundamentals of high and low pressure, of clashing systems, of precipitate formation in relation to the temperature. But these were the things she had learned in school and retained all her life.

Some events still puzzled her, but she thought she preferred it that way. Possibly Montgomery had achieved that degree of acceptance, of internal calm, and was content to know all there was to know and have it not be enough, but this was beyond her; she needed, at times, to be another leaf blown in the storm. Fog, in particular, was an enticing mystery; it came and went as it pleased, always a treat, a lovely deepening of her world, except when she found herself caught in it on a country road at night, remembering that she'd been told to keep her headlights on low beam, finding each time that it didn't much matter, because either way, high or low, she couldn't see far enough ahead to ease her anxiety, or relax just by trying, and so stayed hunched over the dashboard, gripping tightly, trusting that nothing would come monstrous out of the mist, or scurry beneath her wheels.

Montgomery made the first recording of the day but Dave made two, for the eleven o'clock and four o'clock reports. The others, one in the evening and several on the weekend, were apparently shared at random, though Zhao-Wen seemed to get most of the Saturday and Sunday assignments. "Zhao-Wen" was her guess, but she wasn't certain she had it right; the voice was a little low, a bit too soft for the job, quite feminine for all its matter-of-factness, particularly subdued when identifying itself, at the end, before the "next forecast at" announcement that always came last. "Zhao-Wen Shaw" was what it sounded like; she wished she could tell whether it was, in fact, the familiar surname she seemed to hear, or instead a Chinese name that resembled it. If the former, she knew that Zhao-Wen was married, or had been, and to a man from a different background; if the latter, she knew nothing at all. She pictured them all sitting around a long table, in a lunchroom with sandwich and soda and coffee machines—like the one her father had led them to in the basement of the museum, after each Tuesday night lecture, when she was a child, or the one in the daily comic strip about the TV reporter, who sat with his paper cup while the glamorous lady co-anchor importuned him—discussing meteorology and their professional and personal experiences in small towns across America before they came to the big city to work on the weather line. If Zhao-Wen was Zhao-Wen Shaw she probably came down, sometimes, after finishing a tape, to find her husband toying with the yogurt he'd bought with three dropped quarters, talking to someone from maintenance or the typing pool as he waited for her. If she was single, maybe some of the men flirted with her. She was the only woman. To have a companion who understood the solitude, the weight of expectation, was probably something they had all dreamed at night.

She wondered if Montgomery's kindness and concern, unfailingly and cheerfully expressed ("Have a great Wednesday," or "Hope you can get outside to enjoy these unseasonably warm breezes," or, annually, "Let me be the first to wish you and yours a happy and productive new year"), extended to his staff as well as his listeners. She had been calling him for years—it was astonishing that he'd been on the job for so long, through her traumas and changes of direction, through elections and crises and foreign affairs—and had yet to find these statements impersonal or cynical; he was still sincere, still seemed to care what kind of day she had. There were mornings when she woke up, her belly aching, the silence of the apartment a reminder of the vacant places in her life, her doubts, questions that would not be addressed by the things she would do and the people she would meet before she slept again. She remembered how little satisfaction she'd had the day before, how keenly she'd felt the lack of substance, the inadequacy of the steps she might have taken when she was younger—a good lunch, a new paperback, a burst of energy on the job, a note to an old boyfriend—to alleviate her loss, her unfulfilled anticipation. She tried to concentrate on the objects in her home that had weight and meaning, like the grain in the polished wood of the floors or the picture she'd painted one summer in the Berkshires, a gentle scene of hills and sheep and a falling-down hut, but her eyes were drawn instead to the things she wished she could put away from her: poorly made items she'd purchased for next to nothing, unwanted catalogs piling up on the little table in the bathroom, cards from people she'd never had any interest in. On these mornings she wished she were not so steady, that she could be unwell half the time, like the woman she'd shared an office with, who had worked her way through a few extra sick days and then chronic absence to a complete disappearance, unannounced and undiscussed until, finally, their supervisor had explained that she'd gone home to England to enter a hospital, or possibly a "long-term recovery facility," as if she'd had tuberculosis in a novel written in 1893, not some curable illness in a world where those with problems that couldn't be solved were a miserable lot indeed.

On these mornings, it amazed her that Montgomery's well-wishes didn't offend and infuriate her, making her cry because they came from him and not from someone with whom she had lain down the night before, who had gripped and held her, who so warmed the sheets that what she felt was a desperate desire to stay, or to go, instead of indifference at the prospect of exchanging one location for another.

It made her uneasy to be reminded that others called the weather number. A man she met on jury duty, who sat down next to her on the waiting room bench just as she was swinging her heavy bag up onto the empty place so she could find her book, and graciously held it in his lap once he understood what she'd been trying to do, volunteered freely, without her introducing the topic, that he relied "absolutely" on the telephone reports, that he enjoyed calling but that his particular concern was in the winter, because the parking in his neighborhood was difficult and he had a horror—he admitted it was "neurotic" with a frank humor she admired—of not being able to find a place, of circling around and around in the night, cursing the heaped mounds of snow blocking the curb, until he was forced to leave his car in the middle of the street to be towed and then sent by the police to the junkyard where it would be crushed as an abandoned vehicle. He liked to be sure his small yellow hatch-back was "safely tucked away" in some legal, non-snow-emergency space well before the bad weather began, he said, and therefore needed to be in "constant touch" with Montgomery and the rest so he could identify the precise moment at which to park the car and start using buses and taxis, rearranging his life accordingly. After the storm, if it turned out to be a big one, he left the car where it was until the snow had melted enough to return things to normal. Sometimes he needed to take the car out while the parking was still terrible, but he tried to avoid it at all costs; once, he said, his uncle had yelled at him "something awful" for taking the train to the airport to pick him up, rather than driving, shouting "All you care about is your parking place!" in front of the other passengers at the luggage carousel. They talked easily and animatedly about the weather line personalities, and the wind, and what outdoor cats and dogs might do when it was wet and cold and they were shut out of the house, until her name was called. She hoped, a little, though he was quite a bit older, that he would remember it and later look up her number; perhaps if they'd served on a jury together or had a chance to talk further it would have become a friendship, but she never saw him again.

Calling Montgomery was a constant in her life, like Monday night shopping or the bills at month's end, but sometimes, inexplicably, she neglected to do it. Caught in the rain without an umbrella, waiting in front of a restaurant in the cold—she liked to watch for the person she had arranged to meet—in pumps and nylons instead of boots, she was embarrassed and annoyed, knowing she might have avoided discomfort. On business trips or vacations, away from home and ritual, she forgot the forecasts entirely; it almost never occurred to her to call a weather line other than her own, although once, before a camping trip, she dialed the number for a small city near the state park, and was surprised to hear advertisements for local goods and services between one cycle of the report and the next.

On another occasion, visiting her mother's mother in Chicago, she was strangely anxious about whether her return flight would be able to land. She had always worried about leaving O'Hare during the winter months, but having confirmed her departure she remained unsatisfied, eager to find out if it was clear at both ends. Calling the number from Illinois—she had to pause, to think of it—was an odd experience; remembering her grandmother's limited means she used her calling card, and pictured the telltale sequence of digits, whose first two members would have been "WE" in earlier years, appearing on her phone bill weeks later, for the first time, like a charm, like a fingerprint, like a souvenir.

# · This
# Strange
# Shape

DANA raked the leaves carefully. He raked each leaf as if it mattered. There were a lot of leaves, and no matter what he did he would miss some of them, and in any case they were going to end up in plastic bags in the dump, a resting place he wasn't convinced was any better than his yard. But it was the kind of job he couldn't do at all unless he did it thoroughly and meticulously.

The yard was spacious and rectangular. One long edge was bounded by the house, the other by the lot next door, with a low wooden fence in between and enough young trees growing next to it, on either side, to provide some sense of separation and privacy. The same low fence turned the corner to run between the yard and the street.

At the back of the yard was a taller fence, also of wood, belonging to the house on the other side of it. It was a spite fence; it was turned around so that its inside, with the bracing timbers showing, faced Dana's house and yard rather than the property it surrounded, but only for the one section. The people in the house with the spite fence said that a previous owner was supposed to have put it up when a Jew, the first in the neighborhood, moved into what was now Dana's house. That was all anybody knew about it.

All the ground in the rectangle defined by these four edges was covered with grass, but the smaller area behind the house, at the foot of the back door steps, was paved with large, square concrete slabs of an older type. There was also a sandbox, and a patch of bare dirt that Dana had tried several times to seed before giving up. The spite fence started in the back corner of the yard and ended at the wall of the small, blocky garage, now a tool shed, at the end of the driveway, which ran along the far side of the house. Past the driveway—an old one, with twin concrete tracks that were too close together for the station wagon, weeds somehow thriving between them—was a new metal chain-link fence, and on the other side of that was the house of the Mendozas, whose four-year-old played with Dana's children and had only recently begun to try to climb the fence between the yards instead of going around by the front.

The biggest, oldest tree on the lot stood behind the dirt patch, next to the spite fence, spreading its knobby, dark, thickly leaved branches over almost the whole of what the family called the "back" yard. This green ceiling, and the high fence and the garage wall, and the rear of the house—much sheerer than the front, which moved back as it rose through the porch roof and the gables—combined to provide, for Dana, the feel of an outdoor room, protected but fresh. Though it wasn't warm enough to relax outside for long, he planned to take a can of soda to the back yard and sit for a while after he was done with the raking.

Straightening from a crouch as he pulled together the edges of the trash bag he'd just filled, trying to guess how many more he would need, he saw Norma standing on the sidewalk, looking over the fence at him, holding the grips of a small briefcase in her left hand and a bag from the twenty-four-hour store in her right. He was in the middle of the yard, too far from her to speak to her except by raising his voice, and he started toward her but then stopped, tying closed the mouth of the bag and throwing it on the pile at the foot of the big tree before walking in her direction.

"That's a lot of leaves," she said.

"Hi," he said. He was gratified not to be nervous, or even excited in any real sense, but he was also glad that she still appealed to him so definitely. For that reason it would be pleasant to talk with her, no matter what was said. "You look as wonderful as you always have," he told her.

She smiled. "You're as generous as you always were."

"It is a lot of leaves," he said. "Especially when you consider how many trees there are around here. Mine should amount to"—he glanced at the unbagged piles scattered about the yard, and at the leaves he hadn't raked yet—"seven or eight bags, and this isn't even the biggest lawn in the neighborhood. I'd say there will probably be at least twenty thousand bags of leaves raked in this town in the next month or so." He looked at her; she was still smiling brightly, very attentive. "Imagine twenty thousand trash bags full of leaves, all in one place."

"I wish we could still burn them," she said. "I feel bad for the children, that they're missing the smell."

"I haven't been this close to you in over a year," he said.

She shrugged. "It seemed to be the thing to do," she said. "The way to be." He noticed that her outfit was prosperous-looking—not formal, but expensive, well made. Soft and supple. "I didn't want to take halfway measures. It appeared to me to be a matter of deciding, one way or the other."

"I guess I didn't know there was anything to decide," he said.

"That would be another way of putting it."

They stood, Norma with her bags, her skirt touching the fence, Dana with his hands on his hips. He wished he had his rake to lean on but it was in the middle of the yard, where it had fallen when he dropped it, going to get the bag. The house looked beautiful in the afternoon sun; he realized, at last, that his wife had found just the right paint for it, after they'd agonized for weeks (he'd been stunned that there were so many to choose from), bickering about it and even yelling at each other, so despairing of ever finding the perfect shade that they'd considered different colors entirely, like blue and gray, though they were both certain that white was what they wanted.

"I understand your family is well and happy," she said, nodding several times, not really looking anywhere, her eyes almost turned inward, as if she were agreeing with herself. "From what I'm told everything is going very nicely."

"What brings you here now?" he asked.

She smiled again. He was impressed by her ease, her lack of embarrassment; she was self-conscious but not anxious. "The car developed some problems on the highway, so I decided to leave it at the gas station"—she pointed with the briefcase—"and walk home, and when I saw you I realized I couldn't go by without talking to you, without at least looking at you." Their eyes met; as soon as they had, his slid over her face and down her throat to the open neck of her blouse.

"It was easy to avoid making contact with you," she went on, "when I never saw you. Not that it was an accident—I mean, it was easy to arrange to not see you when I didn't know what I was missing."

"Am I that irresistible?" he asked.

"I have an attachment," she said. "I never denied that. I'm very, very attached to you, Dana." They stood, thinking about that, while the wind—it had been an unusually still day, but now the breeze was picking up, and they could hear the tail of the kite that was stuck in the telephone wires, softly flapping—carried some of his unraked leaves around the yard.

"At any rate," she said, "it's possible I chose this route home because your house is on it."

"It's even possible you imagined the car trouble."

"Where's Jodie?" she asked.

"Still at the office, probably," he said.

"And the children?"

"Gymnastics and swimming. She'll pick them up on her way home."

He found himself wanting, oddly, to hold on to the strap of her small handbag as it hung on her left shoulder, resting between her hip and her forearm. He was extremely aware of her form, of her curves—he was extremely aware of memories of cupping her breasts, of pulling at her thighs, of rubbing his cheek on her shoulder—but he didn't want to touch her body, just to keep it from moving away, to anchor it, at least for a minute or two.

"Do you think," she asked, "that she suspected us?"

He smiled, not very warmly. "No," he said. "She didn't."

Norma sighed. "What's her explanation, then, for the fact that we don't socialize anymore?"

"Well, it's very convenient," he said. "She's still surprisingly angry at Marty about the zoning thing. As a matter of fact, during all those months it was only because I insisted—because I wanted to cover for you and me—that we saw you at all. She would have been happy to stop any time, and when you told me you wanted to break it off, I went to her and agreed that Marty had badly overdone it, and admitted that I should have been more supportive of her while it was happening, and so on. And that did the trick."

"I see," she said. "So she never knew at all."

"Not at all," he said.

"That's one term I really can't stand," she told him. " 'Break it off.' I wish you wouldn't use it. It's so violent."

"It seemed pretty violent to me at the time," he said.

"It's so petty. It makes it sound as if I wanted to hurt you."

He reached out then, on the verge of taking the strap of her purse, of tugging on it. She looked at his hand, then back at his face; she might have been angry, or scornful, but she didn't back away, which confused him.

"Norma," he said, "when I say you broke it off, that's pretty much the way it was for me. I was in you all the time. Even when I wasn't in you—when we were lying there talking—I was in you, and even when you weren't there, when I hadn't seen you for days, I was in you." He hesitated for a moment. They were too far from anywhere, and he had been speaking too quietly, for anyone to have heard.

"Even when I was in my own wife, I was in you," he said. She looked down at her shoes, and the sidewalk. "When you said we had to stop, it was like cutting a connection of flesh, or tearing it. I felt like I bled and bled, like I should have had the chance to put on a tourniquet first."

She sighed again. "You didn't say so then," she said.

" 'Breaking it off' is exactly right," he said. "Except it sounds brittle. And quick."

She had stood so uprightly when he first saw her there, so steadily, but now she seemed to droop. "I won't say I haven't had second thoughts," she said.

"It was like nothing else that ever happened to me." Dana wondered at his own animation. He'd assumed he no longer cared. "I don't know if we were in love or not, but I've never been so excited. I've never felt so strong." He lowered his voice, though it was already quite low. "I couldn't believe how good you tasted. How happy we were with everything we tried."

She nodded, twice, slowly, transferring the briefcase to her right hand so she could run her left index finger over the points on the top of the fence.

"All my life I hoped it would be like that," he said.

"Well, me too," she said. "Who didn't?"

His own left hand went to the fence. The wind made him cold. He wouldn't sit in the back yard, even if he finished today.

"I thought I'd died and gone to heaven," she said.

He was careful to say nothing.

"I'll never forget," she said. "But it was getting to be a very big problem."

"Apparently you thought so."

"The point is, that isn't all there is. There are other very important things."

"Such as?"

"Such as fidelity," she said, "and comfort. Responsibility. Knowing your limits."

"I knew exactly where the limits were," he said. "But exactly."

"Perhaps it wasn't as clear to me as it was to you."

"Did you want more than you were getting?" he asked.

"Dana," she said, "as distressing as this may be to hear, there were times when I wanted less." She looked at him. "You men find it easy, after the fact, to think about other things. You go about your business all relaxed, and when you smell it on your fingers you feel excited and proud, and you wash it off if it shouldn't be there. But when I smelled you I would cry."

"You said you liked it."

"Liked it?" She laughed. "Weren't you listening? I loved it. I died for it. But you were right when you said you were in me every single minute. You were, and sometimes you choked me. You hurt me. There was always pain."

He said, "That sounds like something entirely different." A moment before he had wanted, amazingly, to take her into the house with him; he could still feel the warm skin at the neck of her blouse against the palm of his hand, and the beginning of the slope, the rise. Now he was exposed, very cautious, very still, as if he had been suddenly exhausted, and reminded of his age. "That's not the way I remember it," he said.

"Surprise," she said.

She turned and took a step or two along the sidewalk, but then— perhaps realizing that any neighbor, watching through a window, would see her leaving abruptly, firmly, as if displaying passion, as if they had been talking about something very intimate—stopped and faced him again, though she didn't come back to where she had stood before.

"It would be nice," she said, "if the four of us had dinner or drinks some time. I know Marty feels very badly about everything that happened."

He nodded. "It would be nice," he said, "if you remembered how it was for us. How much you wanted me."

"Don't worry about that," she said, turning again. "Don't give it another thought."

"Take care of yourself," he said. He watched her walk away, indifferent and a bit frightened by it, hands on his hips, listening to the wind and leaves, wondering if he had ever really looked at her before, wondering how he could have brought himself to treasure, to touch, to embrace this woman, this strange shape.

# Hall
# of
# Fame

I have trouble deciding how to remember my father. Sometimes, he's like a snowflake, landing on the end of my mitten, fading quickly, vivid. Sometimes he's the front lawn as I come home from school, or a barking dog, or a favorite toy lost far from home.

"I can see why the price was so low," she said. "I wonder about that mattress."

We were in Cooperstown, to visit the Hall of Fame. It was a trip I'd tried for a long time to arrange. The month before I'd mailed a check to Pearce House, listed as a bed and breakfast in the Visitor's Guide, actually a private home with two rooms on the attic floor, rented to tourists for extra income. We saw this in the first few minutes: there were old board games and children's books piled against the wall between the two bedroom doors, and tears in the wallpaper above them, and cartons of clothes in the large hall closet. Next to the banister were brochures and pamphlets for local attractions, neatly laid out on a small wooden table. Our hostess—a small, frail young woman in jeans, a plain sweatshirt, and padded slippers—explained that her two nephews had left earlier in the day, "so you'll have the bathroom all to yourselves."

I sat on the bed. "I've slept on better," I said. I'd chosen Pearce House over the nicer places because the rates were low. Now I worried that Sally might be unhappy, or that Ted and Louise would not enjoy themselves, though I knew they wouldn't blame me. If I admitted my fault they would deny it, and it would change hands, uncomfortably, until Ted made a joke about eventually getting even.

Sally went into the bathroom—a nice place, really, the most appealing room I'd seen, despite the "Bible Verses for Life" pamphlet in a little rack over the sink—and I walked across the landing to the other bedroom, to check on Louise and Ted. He was lying on one of the twin beds, his eyes closed, and she was sitting in a rocking chair, a bit lost in it despite her size, rocking slightly, as if she'd been waiting for some time.

Almost every week now I read in the paper or hear on the radio another story about divorce, and its harsh effects on children and their parents, and ways to reduce the damage, so it becomes harder and harder to appreciate the isolation that my parents (and I) felt when I was a boy. More than half the couples in our affluent, closely knit suburban neighborhood eventually divorced, but my parents were the first. My mother and father always discussed it openly; I learned to tell myself that schoolmates who were greatly surprised to learn that my father didn't live with us just didn't know much about things that happened in the world. I did well in school, and while I suppose that, at the time, even teachers who truly cared about their pupils weren't very eager to get involved with family problems, I believe I rarely called on them to. Even when I cried in front of the other children—it happened as late as the fifth grade, when someone secretly destroyed the maze I'd spent a week building for the class mouse—I'm sure I never mentioned my father's absence, or his fights with my mother. Now, I hope, when children like me insist that everything's fine, their teachers and counselors understand and take pity. But only my mother and sister knew how many of my afternoons I spent reading on my bed.

Although my father made a lot of money there wasn't much to spare. I didn't have family skiing trips and island holidays like my classmates, but I had something as good, or maybe better; the money went instead to my father's apartments, which always contained interesting things, and presents for us. On special occasions—he hardly needed an excuse—he would cook us a meal: hamburgers and pickles and olives and potato chips, with ice cream or some kind of unusual cookies or cake for dessert. It was a standard menu but we never tired of it, and the festive paper tablecloths and napkins and decorations, generally with some colorful centerpiece, added to our pleasure. He was as eager to please my sister and me as he was to please anyone with whom he was still on good terms, and as the years went by and he got farther away from us all, the generous and loyal impulse remained deep, though it applied to fewer and fewer people.

We rarely went into his bedroom. The big blizzard of my childhood started when my sister and I were at his apartment. I remember playing with the dachshund bubble-gum holder while it snowed, and drawing with pastel crayons on the easel, and my father coming in to tell us that he had called my mother (they almost never spoke, and when they did, they fought) and that we were staying with him, on account of the storm. Strangely, considering his preoccupation with having everything we might need, there was no guest bed, or sleeping bags, or even (I think) extra pillows. Ruth and I slept in his bed and he slept on the floor next to us, wrapped in a couple of blankets, in his undershirt and trousers. I was ten. The next morning we helped him shovel out his car, and he took us home.

Walking to town from Pearce House—to get something to eat and then to the Hall—I talked with Louise while the others went ahead. Autumn was almost over. I'd hoped for brilliant leaves but it was too late in the year; if anything, the trees were browner and barer once we crossed the state line and passed Albany. The town was lovely anyway as we went along the road, looking at the lake on the other side and the old, grand buildings on its shore, and then turned and passed some of the places where we could have stayed, and the neatly kept private homes. Cooperstown made me yearn, immediately, for the early days of the century and a communal life, despite the knowledge that small towns are often much too small, that my parents, for instance, would have been trapped. As I looked around me I saw the old houses and the big trees and lawns and pretended to forget about problems like theirs. I wanted to belong, or to play at belonging; we'd come in the off-season and missed the crowds, and if I ignored the cars parked almost everywhere I could imagine simplicity, and knowing everybody, a different pace and a sense of ease.

Louise said she'd found an excellent guitar to give to Ted for his birthday.

"He'll tell you you shouldn't have."

She smiled. "He's different with me," she said.

"I got Sally a Celtics jacket," I said. Sally's birthday was a few days before Ted's.

"Isn't that nice," said Louise. "She'll be so pleased."

"When I picked out the fanciest model the man said, 'She'll love you for this,' and I said, 'Why do you think I'm getting it?'"

"Isn't that nice," Louise said again.

Sally stopped, looked back, pointed ahead, asking; I nodded, though I wasn't sure. "You know, I was in the store, across from the park, and one of the ballplayers was there, buying up souvenirs to take home to Tennessee or somewhere, I guess. They were all talking and I joined in, and I was dying to tell Sally about it— discussing baseball with a big-leaguer!—but I knew I'd end up stumbling. I was so sure I'd spoil the surprise that I just kept quiet."

We wanted to go to a lunchroom recommended by the Pearce House proprietor's husband. We could get breakfast there any time, he'd said. We turned the corner onto the main street and found it easily; though it wasn't yet noon the booths were full, and we had to wait. Louise and I ate fried eggs and toast, and Ted had an omelet, and Sally ordered a hamburger, which I finished for her. The men behind us talked about a fishing trip; others gossiped and read the paper. I was sure the diner wasn't in the pamphlets and brochures outside our rooms at Pearce House. I was quickly fond of it, forever attached.

My father was a charming man, generous and kind, as long as you were still in his favor. He loved conversation and company, and fun, and he needed to establish a sense of rich enjoyment, wherever he was.

There are no photographs of him on my walls, but I do have a small reproduction of a painting (or a detail of a painting) by Degas. It shows an elegant gentleman (perhaps a boulevardier?) from the right side and a bit to the back and above, a slightly uneasy angle, with little that can be distinguished in the background (I think he is standing on a broad sanded walk, in a park, near a tree). He has longish brown hair, though he is balding, and a full red beard. His right hand is raised in front of him, at the level of his shoulder, as though he has just drawn on the cigarette it holds. He may be gesturing to someone out of the frame to the right, but I prefer to think he is alone, content with his own companionship. His left foot is set farther out than his right, pointed almost as much to the side as to the front, and his left hand rests on the back of his left hip, holding his hat upside down, as if, upon finishing the cigarette, he might bring it around to the front and discover that, a minute before, someone had desposited in it a surprise or treat. He looks very much like my father, and so like me.

During the time I was with him as an adult—a space of a few months before he died—even strangers would notice how much we resembled one another. (Once, on a trip to New Orleans in the late 1960s, we were wearing the same shirt, a green and blue Greek fishing jersey with pockets, and a young man with long hair turned to his friend and said, "Oh look—twins.") He still had his beard, which I remembered him starting years before, and I had one too by that time, even that being similar to his in the way it refused to fill the space under my prominent lower lip (like his) and connect to the ends of my mustache. There were differences—differences that are disappearing as I age—but the likeness, of gesture and motion as much as of appearance, more noticeable in the flesh than in photographs, was remarkable, and friends, colleagues, and class-mates we happened upon were quick to mention it. I usually left the talking almost entirely to him, embarrassed in advance by the comments and the questions that were asked about this son who had suddenly appeared from nowhere and who could miss it and I didn't know you had children!

My father was at his best in these chance encounters, lively and articulate with a joke for everyone. There are many things I don't like to remember about him, but I do like to think of him when I look at the painting of the French man, with rumpled too-long trousers, who may be in conversation or, instead, may be feeling a self-sufficient rightness about the park, the beautiful weather, and his cigarette, confident that he will soon be with someone, either an acquaintance who will happen along (since his friends share his tastes and will be equally eager to enjoy the day), or a stranger, possibly a mother to whose daughter he will present a small toy.

As a child, my "regular" life—the experiences and people I shared with my playmates, my daily routine, all the things I could connect in a way that made sense to a boy of six or eight or ten—didn't involve him very much. Even the few trips we went on and the Sunday outings and the restaurants (except for festive meals he rarely cooked for us) didn't come up much in waiting-for-the-bus and recess and after-school conversation. I suppose in this way I avoided some of the questions and looks.

One incident I do remember is my first Little League tryout. My father, like me, was never athletic—it was his younger brother who played sports and got mostly Bs and rarely caused his parents concern—but he readily understood how much it would mean to me to be on a team. He canceled his patients for the afternoon and came with me.

Considering how disastrous the tryout was, he didn't involve himself much. He watched from the foul lines as they pinned numbers on our backs and sent us up to hit. As soon as I took my stance, the coaches started telling me I was crowding the plate. Maybe I didn't know what that meant—I didn't know much about baseball then—but more likely I'd gotten into the state in which I sometimes found myself: unable to interpret adult commentary, requiring explicit instruction instead. I was unresponsive, and they were probably pretty annoyed with me; eventually, my father spoke up and told me to move back slightly and turn away from the pitcher. Peter Finch, an older boy from our neighborhood who was one of the stars of his team, was on the mound, and while I got my bat on every one of the first three or four pitches he threw, they were all weak grounders. From some unknown place, in front of all those men and boys, I summoned the courage—I still marvel—to tell Peter to "slow it down a little." He shouted back that he was already throwing as slowly as he could. I missed the next two, then hit another ground ball and then on the last pitch a one-hopper to short, relieved to have made solid contact as I ran to first base. (I did remember not to throw the bat.)

Fielding was next. I chose a place near the second baseman's position and almost instantly had my one good moment of the tryout. A coach hit a line drive immediately to my left, about head-high, and I managed to leap and knock it down with my glove. One of the other coaches even shouted something approving while I was having a lot of trouble picking the ball up to throw it to first.

My only other chance was a medium bouncer right at me. It tied me up completely; the ball got stuck between my glove and the ground, and I knocked it behind me, and instead of turning around I tried to back up, kicking it with my heel so it stayed behind me. When I finally managed to grab it my throw went past first base. I was strangely unembarrassed; I may have smiled. Kevin Something, a boy I knew slightly from school, said "Nice pickup," and I think I chose (though I knew better) to take it as a compliment, as if it had been another difficult play and I'd again done well just to keep it in the infield.

I don't think my father had much to say afterwards—how I wish I had seen him talking to someone as he watched!—and I had little trouble convincing myself that I'd done well enough, that there were a lot of teams and a lot of places on them. Even when I got the letter I didn't feel too badly, but when I heard they'd taken Art Goldstein—with whom I'd spent many hours, years before, drawing pictures of soldiers and tanks and planes—I was distraught. My mother only made it worse by explaining that Art, who I knew was no better than I was, had gotten in because his uncle, Peter Finch's father, was coach of the team that had chosen him.

Years later, when I made another fine play with a lot of people watching—in a game between my department and some salesmen, in which I also had three hits, I (playing second still) dove for and snared, backhanded, a hard shot to my right and, lying on the dirt, found the ball in my glove and tossed quickly and accurately to

Marvin Karp at shortstop, who threw (just as quickly and accurately) to first to complete the double play and get us out of a tough inning— I thought of that tryout, and Kevin, and my father's look of concern.

When you enter the Hall, the first thing you see—even before you go through the turnstile, if you are eagerly looking ahead—is a statue of Babe Ruth, in his batting stance, in the entrance hall. Ted commented on the size of his hands. It was true; while the statue was about as big as Ted, convincingly life-sized, the hands seemed impossibly large to me. I wondered if Ruth had felt, on first taking up a bat, that it fit perfectly, that he had somehow been born to hold it.

I went to get a map, to plan our visit, but as I looked it over Louise wandered in the Great Moments gallery and Ted started to drift away as well, though Sally was still with me. I often worry about getting to what I really want to see, but I was so pleased to be at the Hall that it was easy, for once, to put my concerns aside.

In fact, Ted and I saw almost everything before we were through. He was unusually restless, moving to the next display before finishing with the one we were looking at, then moving back. Louise and Sally—both baseball fans, Louise for years, in sympathy with her father, who almost made the Boston Braves in the late forties (not long before they moved to Milwaukee), Sally more recently, having learned to love the game since first coming to the park with me that spring—talked between themselves more than to us, as if reluctant to interrupt our thoughts and discussion. They left after two hours or so, agreeing to meet us back at the house, but we had to stay, because it was baseball and history, mixed passion for us both; almost everything we saw held our interest, and gave us pleasure.

I'm jealous, always, of the baseball fans who enjoyed the sport in the old days, before the war, when the same sixteen teams played the same game in the same parks, year after year, under the same sun. Given the pace and shock of change in the twentieth century it's remarkable, even astounding, to think of how stable those baseball decades were; something to rely on and know the rules of, to know the players, to keep track. There was change, of course—the Black Sox and Kenesaw Mountain Landis, the home run discovered, the passing of the spitball and games under lights—and dullness too, but I yearn for those days, and I always root, when my team is not involved, for the other old clubs still playing in the cities in which they started: the Detroit Tigers, the Pittsburgh Pirates, the White Sox, the Reds. Who are the Seattle Mariners?

The exhibits that brought me to those times were a joy. The uniforms were very real. A Washington Senators outfit just like Walter Johnson wore!—and you could tell that some man, or men, had worn it; it looked used, no Disneyland artifice. I was surprised at the lavender and pink in those baseball suits, and was tempted to revise my picture of the past—we so often see it in black and white—until I realized I was looking at the residue of deeper red and blue dyes, manufactured seventy years ago or more, faded by time.

If you go back too far you can lose the thread. The oldest things— many of them in the basement—meant less to us. The gloves were small and useless, the bats so heavy and awkward and strangely shaped, and the sepia men, with their fancy mustaches, appeared to be from another land. We agreed that there were too many exhibits in the Hall, too many cases filled with equipment used in this play or by that player. There are just so many baseballs you can look at before they're all the same.

But the Hall of Fame itself, its bronze plaques bearing the faces of players—some looking happy to be remembered—didn't disappoint us. We studied every plaque, and Ted, who I'd thought was losing interest, came alive again, offering more stories and numbers and shrewd evaluation than I could take in.

It's hard to know how to feel about the teams that have moved, some more than once. The Braves were the first to leave, starting a trickle and then a flood of baseball migration, a wandering that hasn't stopped. At times I look on the travelers with affection or sympathy, as vessels of the past, though I don't know that they have any real connection to it. I tried to be pleased when the Oakland A's—née Philadelphia and then Kansas City—returned, officially, to the name Athletics, and hoped that a few old men in Fishtown were pleased as well. But it didn't give them their team back.

The stadiums used by those teams are all gone now, as are many others whose former tenants play in newer, bigger, shinier parks across town or in the suburbs. They could have been saved and even used for other purposes, but those who loved them, in the intolerable pain of abandonment, had to destroy them, leaving no reminder. Once torn down they couldn't be raised again.

In one gallery we saw a picture of Shibe Park in Philadelphia, packed with fans for a big game, the rooftops beyond the outfield fence lined with men in straw hats. I was talking about the game as a rite of continuity, about my delighted understanding, on walking to the park, that others had come to the same place to do the same thing for the same reasons two generations before, when I noticed a man listening and nodding agreement. He came closer and said he remembered seeing games at Shibe as a child. His family stood by, ill at ease I thought, as I talked more about the old parks, a little embarrassed, and about the shame of letting them pass away. (Shibe was still standing not long ago; there's a terribly sad picture of the field full of weeds, a tree growing out of the pitcher's mound.)

At the end we visited the gift shop. We bought some things, including a beer glass for George, who'd wanted to come with us, and a Braves mug for Louise's father. I thought about getting a few of the reproduced caps of vanished teams—the Brooklyn Dodgers, the St. Louis Browns—but as I stood, holding one in my hand, I saw that they were really and truly gone, and I put it back.

I'd expected to be troubled, at the Hall, by reminders of my own team's tribulation, its lack of triumph, but it happened only once, in the shop, when I looked at the shelves of World Series steins— one for each year, with the logo of the winning team, and the rosters of winners and losers both—and had to go decades back to find one with our name on it. And then it seemed to matter much less than it had.

My father's generosity—remembered fondly by so many—often went too far. On almost any excuse he would shower us with gifts, and when he dropped us off after a birthday visit we would walk up the driveway lugging trash bags full of presents. It annoyed and frustrated my mother, who had to deny us things. We knew she was right from an early age; my father was excessive, clearly so, and aside from the burden of comparison it placed on her my mother genuinely thought all those gifts were bad for us. I think she even understood that it made us ashamed of him, something she regretted and perhaps feared.

Nor was my father always indulgent. He was often stern, even irrationally punitive. He could be unaccountably angry about very small things, and at times he became frighteningly enraged. There are certain episodes—the "faithless daughter" lecture at the skating rink, the last two days of a trip to New York, during which he would not speak to me—that my sister and I will never, ever be able to think of without tears, although he always apologized later. When we talk (and sometimes joke) about those times, Ruth and I are in a private reserve of painful and still inexplicable memory in which no one, not even my mother, will ever join us.

He was such an unmixed man, or rather, he was very mixed, but it became apparent only over time, if you knew him very well. At a given moment he was either warm or ice cold, the image of reason or unrestrained. The kind, loving person was much more evident than the other, of course, and this is how most people thought of him. It did me no good to feel angry at those who, after his death, approached me, some buttonholing me on the street, to tell me how much he'd meant to them, what a wonderful teacher and admirable practitioner and good friend he'd been, how fascinating his conversation, how fine it must have been for me to have a father like that. The pointlessness of answering overwhelmed me, and I could never in any case have explained or even described the strange combination of contradictory paths he followed. I know my father always wanted children, and that he cherished us, but he was wholly unprepared; he didn't know what to do with us, or even who we really were.

My father had close friends who had two boys, and we visited them regularly. I can remember the living room of their duplex across the river, and the mynah bird they had for years, who would say a few words if you coaxed her long enough (it made my sister laugh). Ray, born three years before me, was a tall, muscular boy, always on Little League teams. One day he announced with pride that he'd made the majors. I thought I understood that Ray—maybe he was four years older than me, he was so large—was actually playing for the New York Mets. I remember turning the TV on to find a Mets game and telling my mother that Ray would be up to bat at any moment. She knew Ray and how old he was, and her gently expressed doubt that he would be playing on television only made me more certain. I insisted that I knew what I was talking about, that it was wrong for her to question me.

A week or two later we were all visiting the zoo or a park; as I walked with my father, behind the others, I told him about watching the game, and wondered why I hadn't seen Ray. He listened silently. Eventually Ray came back to join us; he was amazed, of course, and amused—to his credit, he did much less than he might have to humiliate me; he was probably flattered—and ran off, yelling, "Hey

Dad! Guess what Davie thought!" Even then my father said nothing. Why didn't he tell me the truth? What was the source of this strange betrayal?

Ted and I returned to Pearce House to find Louise and Sally drinking tea in the kitchen. We decided to wait an hour or so before going out to dinner. Everyone seemed happy. Sally and I lay comfortably on the bed, in each other's arms, and talked about the Hall, and Louise and Ted, and where we would spend Thanksgiving. It was very quiet, an advantage after all of Pearce House over more frequented places, and in the October twilight, in the resting time, the room's scarred, faded wallpaper and battered furnishings looked almost like home.

Eventually I reached for the catalog I'd brought from the gift shop at the Hall—forcing Sally to turn on the bedside lamp, which I regretted—and we leafed through it. In my anxiety I'd marked a place. Birthdays are important to me. As I once managed to say to someone (discovering the fact, in a moment, as I might have bent down to pick up a stone on the beach), I seem to believe I was never told, as a child, that anybody was glad I'd been born. This couldn't have been true, but it's a persistent conviction I've come to accept, if only because it refuses to leave me; I remain, like my father, compelled to mark the birthdays of all my friends with a gift or a card or a call, making elaborate plans, wondering what surprises my own will bring.

On my first birthday with Sally I saw she hadn't understood, had had no way of knowing. After her birthday she might. I kept us moving through the catalog, and when we came to the pages of team jackets I pointed and said, "I'm going to get you one of those," and when she said, "What I really want is a Celtics jacket," it thrilled me, and it made me sad.

• • •

Now that my father is gone, what I have is the places he used to take us to, the sights he pointed out. When I left, briefly, for another city, in a distant state, it was partly because I had come to find their presence—some only in memory—difficult, and needed surroundings without his stamp. The park where he took us to play, with the streams and the bridges off of which we would drop sticks, racing to the other side to see them emerge; the Indian restaurant, replaced now by a big hotel, with its elaborately carved elephant tusk in a glass case in the lobby; "the crazy man's house," decked with strings and strings of lights on the walls and the trees and bushes, and a lighted Santa Claus with sleigh and reindeer and a big sack of presents on the roof, from Thanksgiving into January; these were reminders of him. I wanted to keep them, but I needed to be free.

Somewhere between my return and Sally they became easier to bear. At first I pursued them, inviting friends to the astronomy lectures, still going on, to which he'd taken us on the third Thursday of each month (where I pleased and embarrassed him—no children under six allowed—by shouting the answer to a question), pointing them out at every turn, but eventually I made peace.

For a number of years the crazy man, or at least his displays, went away. The house was dark at Christmas, no different from its neighbors. Then, not long ago, he was suddenly back, though it wasn't the same; there were a few lights, and a wreath, and a Santa (not the lighted one) on the lawn, and I was pleased to see that though he had abandoned his extravagance, he had never really been gone, and had found a way to let us know it, if less dramatically, perhaps more in keeping with his advancing years.

When we went to their room, to say we were ready to eat, we heard music, and opened the door to find that Ted had taken a guitar—a small, old one, but with a nice sound—from the closet. We sat with them, delaying our meal, though we knew the restaurants would be crowded on a Saturday night.

"Play the one you wrote for me," asked Louise. She blushed, but with a lovely smile, and Ted, embarrassed as well, caught, played the song without further request—it was night by now, full darkness outside the window, and that and the rocking chair I was sitting in coaxed from me another rush of comfort—and without looking at any of us:

> *I thought I wanted to be a star,*
> *I thought I wanted a fancy car,*
> *I thought I wanted to drink champagne,*
> *I thought I wanted shelter from the rain,*
> *But all, all, all I really wanted was you.*
> *Yes, all, all, all I really wanted was you.*

Sally smiled too; I was glad she was able to. If Ted could say it, I was pleased to listen.

> *I thought I wanted to win a prize,*
> *I thought I wanted X-ray eyes,*
> *I thought I wanted to get ahead,*
> *I thought I wanted to stay in bed,*
> *But all, all, all I ever wanted was you.*
> *Yes, all, all, all I really wanted was you.*

I wondered, how does he know?

Six weeks or so later, going through the papers piled on my desk, deciding that I had kept this offer or that appeal long enough, or that it would have to stay in the pile, I came across a flier for the batting cage at Cooperstown, near the Hall of Fame, which I'd wanted to visit but hadn't because it was closed for the season. I imagined myself, wearing a batting helmet, taking my stance against a ninety-mile-per-hour fastball, and eventually—after convincing Sally to change one more dollar bill and feed the quarters into the box, with Ted's encouragement, and Louise's cautions that I not get any part of me in the way of a pitch—tensing at just the right moment, anticipating the path of the ball, and hitting it, finally, cleanly to right.

# · The Way
# She Tells
# Him Dreams

SOMETIMES she speaks in a way that upsets him. It stirs in him anxiety, or fear. He can't stop her; she speaks automatically, in a flood, with steady emphasis, placing "and" or "then" or some other short sound between each pair of phrases so that they run together to make not sentences but an uninterruptible, undiscussable string of words. The words come quickly and she's distracted as she says them, and won't look at him directly. Even when he grasps the meaning there's a vague quality to the way she conveys it, a lack of structure and purpose. She seems not to care but the manner of her speech belies this. There is something urgent about it. It's as if she believes she can force him to listen without listening herself; she can say what she has to say without acknowledging her need.

At first he thought it upset him because he felt disregarded. Then he decided it was because he had no opportunity to question, or reply. He now understands that what he wants to run from is the burden it places on him. He is a captive audience to her tales.

She speaks this way when she tells him her dreams. She has dreams, he knows, almost every night, but describes them to him infrequently. There is never anything in her account to show why this particular dream is important, why it must be told, and the unnatural way in which she speaks deprives him of the usual clues in her voice, which is generally expressive, the stresses and pauses and changes of speed that would tell him, if they were there, what actually mattered.

In the past he tried to discuss the dreams with her. Now he knows better, and even when he sees her distress and makes plans to approach her in the evening, to comfort her, he can't remember when he tries a single detail of what she told him, even an hour later, as if he's taking her at her word and they are playing together a game of pretending she's said nothing at all.

He remembers one description that was very brief. "I dreamed we had a castle," she told him. As he waited for her to say more she continued to pack for the trip they were taking.

"Is that all?" he asked, after moments of silence.

She shook her head. "A castle," she said, "high on a hill."

When they part in the morning he goes to work on foot and his route takes him past familiar places, through a wide range of separate environments like the back lot of a movie studio: residential streets, light industry, a historic site, railroad tracks, small research laboratories, parking garages, a massive storage warehouse, lunchrooms, a college campus, office towers, vacant lots. There are days when he feels it's too long a walk but on the whole he's grateful for it. He would leave himself notes along the way if he could.

Sometimes she responds to everything he says with a faint hesitation, barely detectable but very definite, so clearly genuine and personal that it causes him to question her affection and regard. Like many experiences from day to day it stimulates in him doubts about himself, but it's more than a reflex; he is convinced at these times that she will eventually leave him. He refuses to ask why though he knows she would tell him, or try to. She would reassure him, but that isn't what he wants. He wants to examine her reservations. He would rather understand.

He apologizes to her more than he feels he should and worries about where this might be leading. It seems he is about to reach a crisis of confidence, but he never does; he is strangely content. She has her own worries, he knows, and some of them concern him.

She likes to tell him about her girlhood. His guess is that it makes her calm. "I imagined I was a Moslem's wife," she says to him as they wait on a porch on a humid day, too rooted to stand and go to lunch, hardly moving.

"A Moslem's wife?" he asks.

She smiles at him. "I was married to a Moslem," she says, "in a Moslem country. At home together we were ourselves, the same as when we dated, in Chicago. Our friends would come for dinner and I would wear a skirt and we would serve them liquor. Cocktails." She smiles again.

"At what age?" he asks.

"Twelve," she says, "and after." He nods, listening.

"When he was at work, or visiting his brothers," she explains, looking at him with intent, with serious eyes, "I was completely alone in another world. Our house was a harem. When I went out I wore a veil and no one could see my face. The women who walked past me never knew I wasn't like them, that under the black cloth was an American woman, not a believer, with a different heart, who covered herself by choice." Her hand is on his arm.

"By necessity," he says.

"By choice," she tells him, distant now.

He has dreams of his own. Their still, aching quality, he senses, keeps them separate from hers; he never tells her about them, though he feels this is wrong. One morning he knows, suddenly, that the night before—and maybe the night before that, it's the kind of dream that seems to have started at some unfindable place, beyond the limits of memory—he dreamed at length about an infant who needed care but was left alone. He lies beside her in the dawn and looks at the ceiling, then at her; he shakes his head.

Sometimes he is clever and capable; sometimes he is clumsy and stupid. The change is not predictable and he is at its mercy. He knows the effect is private, not visible to others, a product of his inner life, but it's so real to him that he tends to abandon the distinction, allowing himself to be led. In his search to comprehend it—he sees himself as a strange weather vane, mounted on a peak, turning this way and that with no choice of his own—he realizes, reluctantly, that he revolves around her; whatever the forces that change him and change him back again, from one face to another, she is at the center, not part of him but his pinion, his anchor, his most vital landmark. She has somehow become the axis of his life.

No matter how he is altered her regard seems not to be, and this frustrates and disappoints him. Is there nothing he can do to remake himself in her eye? Is her attachment to him something she owned before they met, something she claimed and took possession of before he had the chance to build it or tear it down or try to shift its course? How can she be with him, so close to him, for hours and days and not see what he's going through? How can she love him when she doesn't know he's there?

One afternoon he arrives to find her gone. He doesn't know what tells him this—the house is as they left it and he has no reason to believe she won't be home in a minute or five or ten, as expected, gripping a book she borrowed from a friend—but his conviction is deep. He reminds himself to take a breath; standing by the mirror he does and sees he didn't need to. He is calm. As he looks in his own eyes he takes another, and another. He wonders what will happen, what may never be said.

Walking around the block he sets a careful pace. His feet avoid the cracks. He considers buying the cigarette he hasn't had in years. When he returns to find her hairbrush on the bed, to hear her in the shower, he wants to declare a victory but he has no audience; he wants to raise his hands.

Living with her is a burden of unwieldy emotion, an exercise in carrying through, the difference—where there is one—between an interesting time and getting something done. There is little to be sure of. When he's pressed to extremes it never seems to panic him, when he isn't he wonders why. At night, when he is not immediately at rest, he tries to bring sleep by clearing his mind, as he used to, but he can't; the blankness won't come. Night after night he gives up, goes to the window, turns around to see her there, inescapable. She is content in her sleep in a way that confuses and dismays him, but seems almost right; he goes to her and kisses her and she does not wake.

Sometimes, he looks at her with inarticulate joy.

# · The
# Passing
# of Time

PETER has dreams about the women in his life, one at a time or several together. Sometimes his wife Nina joins them; often she does not. The women in these dreams are the warm, affable women who've known him a long time, who genuinely like him and are always glad to see him. Though they may, over the years, have entertained thoughts of making love to Peter, they are now very happy with their husbands and would not be available under any circumstances. Most have young children. When he sees them he wants to hold them; he wants to hear them laugh.

Nina, too, has a young child, hers and Peter's. She lies with it in the big bed in the back bedroom of their third-floor apartment, in the triple-decker they own. The baby takes milk; Nina's eyelids drop and the corners of her mouth turn. Nina has full breasts, brown like the rest of her. Though Peter has always admired and been excited by the color of his wife's skin, the women in his dreams are mostly pale.

The baby, Louis, sucks contentedly, and Nina is contentedly sucked. She is enjoying everything about the situation. Peter comes home from his job as a coach at the high school to find her on the bed, the baby on her stomach, mouth moving on her breast, little hand clutching the edge of her terry cloth robe. When he appears in the doorway she seems to want him—she shifts restlessly—but never enough to move Louis and get up. The baby, after all, is changing everything, as was widely predicted; he seems always to be between them.

One chilly morning, having called in sick, Peter overhears his wife in the driveway, talking to the first-floor tenant's boyfriend. "I hope I didn't make too much noise last night," she says. "I didn't notice anything," says the boyfriend. "The baby was crying," Nina tells him, "and the window was stuck. I guess I got kind of vocal before I realized what time it was." Peter doesn't remember this. Is she really embarrassed? Has she thought he might be listening? "Didn't notice a thing," says the boyfriend.

Nina is technically on leave from her job, but she doesn't like it anymore and they are losing patience with her; everyone knows she won't be back. Nina is a grant administrator for a small foundation that could never find the right recipients before she arrived. Until the baby came she spent long days sifting through proposals, searching out worthy organizations and checking their expenditures, going to endless meetings and seminars to learn about issues and causes; she was rewarded with no computer of her own, standing orders not to use the fax machine, and absurd criticism of the way she dressed and the hours she kept. The staff despised each other generally and Nina most of all, because she clarified their failings.

"Honey," his wife calls out from the back bedroom, at regular intervals, "could you bring me some tea?" Or, "Could you bring me the baby's blanket?" Or a sandwich or the newspaper or the letter from his brother. Once she interrupts his preparation of his special spaghetti sauce—"I'm not hungry, I ate all day" she says— with a request for four separate items it takes him some time to find; when he comes in with his arms full and sits on the edge of the bed, she sees his face and laughs and says, "Honey, look, I'm having the time of my life and I admit it. I wish I could fix it for you too." Then she presses his hand to her thigh.

Ever since they met, Peter has wanted Nina to be more casual, less presentational and stiff, more relaxed and earthy and confident, but now that she is he's not sure he likes it. He finds it unsettling. He wishes they could go back to the days when she wouldn't answer the door without looking in the mirror first; now she just slings the baby onto her hip and marches down the stairs. Even with all the conventions and meetings he never worried about other men, because he knew she wouldn't plan or think about such a thing before the fact, and she never did anything she hadn't prepared for. Now she seems ready for anything. Usually when he gets home from work he lets himself in to find her on the bed with the baby, or on the couch with the baby, or eating something and reading the newspaper in the kitchen, but one afternoon, as he is taking the letters from the mailbox on the porch, the door opens and there she is, in her white bathrobe, with her broad, rounded hips. She looks so exciting that he slams the door closed and takes her there on the stairway; she is pleased and amused to be wanted that badly. He is terribly afraid that some confident man—the tenant's boyfriend, for instance—will ring the bell and be overwhelmed by his good fortune in finding this gorgeous creature, will try furiously to seduce her, baby or no. He has never worried about Nina before, but there is no denying that she seems ready for anything.

On the face of it, Nina has more to worry about than he does; he is surrounded five days a week by fifteen-, sixteen-, and seventeen-year-old girls, most of whom admire him and even think he's cute. Many are almost irresistibly appealing, and they want to make him like them. Not that he would as much as think of looking sideways at any of them; it could be worth his career, his marriage, and his name to give even a single one the impression that he was in pursuit, and he knows that involvement with a girl who, however beautiful, would be unable to hold his interest in conversation for more than a few minutes would never be worth it. Maybe for some men—he has friends who seem willing, even eager, to risk almost anything for a little pleasure of that kind—but not for him.

The girls do, however, keep him in an almost constant state of vague arousal, fertile ground for his frequent thoughts about adventures with women of his own age. He feels very committed to his marriage, he remains truly excited by Nina—she is so exotic, so different from his family and the people he knew, so much the kind of woman he used to see on the street and think "She could never be mine" that he occasionally wants to clap his hands or dance when he remembers that she is actually his wife—and though he isn't sure just how she would react, the prospect of hurting her is very distressing. But he can't shake the idea that it would be a lot of fun and wouldn't be wrong to enjoy a single experience with the right woman: someone happily married, like him, someone who doesn't want to fall in love, who wants to disturb nothing, who would be warm but not too close, who would be satisfied with the one encounter. A person in need of something private, something to call her own.

"Who do you see during the day?" he asks her. "Nobody," she says. "My sister. The people in the market. Denise. Almost nobody. I have to start getting out more." She sighs. "The truth is I'm a little lonely. It can't be good for Louis either."

"I'm here most of the time," he says. "Not really, honey," she says, with a hint of correction. "I know the hours at school probably fly by for you, but they're pretty long for me." He fingers his first-quarter student reports. "I thought you were enjoying it," he says. "I am, but it's getting a little old," she says. "I think I'll take Louis downtown tomorrow and do some shopping."

After she has gone to sleep—after he stands over the crib and watches his son's chest rise and fall, wondering how fast a baby should breathe—he settles on the couch with the photo albums, some hers, one his, several theirs together. Though it's late and he has an early soccer practice, he looks at every page, every face.

Studying the images, he tries to determine if something fundamental has shifted since Nina became pregnant, since she gave birth. He tries to decide where the dream women are coming from, why he loves them so readily. He has had dreams like these all his life, dreams in which everything is easy, in which something he finds himself wanting badly is available in a simple, nearly effortless way (like turning his head, or closing his eyes) that takes the edge of desperation off his desire, so he wakes feeling calm and fulfilled. But he can't be sure whether he had this particular kind before Louis was born, the kind in which women he can't have—he can convince himself that it isn't wholly unrealistic to think that he might have one of them someday, but he knows he won't—are available to him, and want him in return, and no one is harmed when he takes them, no one is the wiser.

He tries to recall the night he thought the skinny, older camp counselor was going to lead him to her cabin and end his frustration. He marches through his past, casting about for triumphs. Remembering a photograph taken just after they met—Nina stands in the midst of her friends, before a college football game, while he watches her from the edge with a possessiveness to which he isn't yet entitled—he finds the empty page on which he knows it was fixed and stays up even later, looking for it in every box and drawer.

The next day, doing errands at lunch, in a hurry, he rounds a corner and almost runs into Martha, who used to teach at his school but left, when she had her second child. He hasn't seen her since Christmas, and he notices, with apprehension, that she is definitely aging—her auburn hair is shot with gray, her face shows wrinkles, she seems less vigorous than he remembers—but still she appeals to him. Unexpected urgency ties his tongue; she drops her shopping bag on the sidewalk, throws her arms around him, and kisses his cheek.

"How are you?" he asks. "Well," she says, stepping back. "And you?" In his searching eyes, she sees something she knows; she lets go of him, smiles and shakes her head; she touches his hand.

Sometimes, making love to Nina, he feels like a stranger, he finds himself remembering a lord's house in Scotland: the wide lawn with fountains, the sunlit terraces overlooking the sea, the framed photograph of the family that lived there, before they gave it to the National Trust. Sometimes, when he is cuddling Louis, or giving him a bath, he tells himself that though Louis came from Nina's body, he isn't going back; though he sucks at her breast and stays close to her all day, he is not her creature, but a separate person whom Peter will come to know.

As he nears the front door, as he comes up the stairs and through the apartment, he notices that what belongs to them, everything, has their permanent mark on it; he would recognize it anywhere. "How was your expedition?" he asks. "Great," she says, grinning, rising off the bed, coming out of the bedroom to embrace him. "It was a breeze." "Did you buy much?" he asks. He sits to rub his aching knee. "I loved being seen with Louis," she tells him. "I loved being a young mother. Everyone smiled at us."

"That's nice," he says. Fingers on his knee, eyes moving over the mug of cold tea, the notepad, the coupons that clutter the table, he looks up to find his wife's back, open to him, vulnerable and real, as though she trusted him completely, as though he had her life in his hands.

"No, really," she says. "Will you come with me soon? I want them to see us all together."

EVERY day, or every other, she was out in the back yard, taking in the sun. Every day, trying to stop himself, failing, he watched her. He stood at his bedroom window—a step back from the glass so she wouldn't see him, though she never looked up—and watched her read her book or magazine and sip from a plastic tumbler of juice or lemonade, or sometimes sunbathe, or sometimes recline on her lounger, half sitting and half lying, motionless, her eyes open, fixed on something on the back porch of her house that he couldn't see. When she did this he found himself oddly relaxed and he too was immobile, at rest, as if he were following her instruction or example, reassured by her stillness and her calm.

He lived on the top two floors of a small house. Her apartment was on the ground floor of the larger house next door. Larger but lower: it had just two stories, and when he looked from his attic bedroom window he could see its roofing shingles and chimneys, and past them to the office building and the broadcasting tower by the shore of the river, and beyond those to the water tank on the distant hillside, where the sun brilliantly set. When he looked down one story from his bedroom or directly across from his living room or kitchen he saw the windows that belonged to Uwe, the man who owned the house, who put the trash out at the same time he did and with whom he exchanged brief greetings. There was a basement apartment on the side nearest him, in addition to Uwe's and the one below it; with the two on the other side there were five in all, in which there lived at least eight people including one small child. When Uwe put the trash out the extent of it was startling, a small mountain range of barrels and bags in front of a pretty blue house on a shaded street. He sometimes wanted to see what was in them but Uwe was meticulous, and always made sure that the lids and knots were tight.

In his house there were just him and Buck, his landlord. Buck had three rooms and he had three: Buck had a living room under his living room and a kitchen under his kitchen, and a bedroom built out where the back porch had once been, and a new back porch built out behind that. He had no porch, but he had the height and the sunlight of his upper stories, and his views to the river and the hill beyond. He had free use of the back yard, though he rarely took advantage of it. Buck loved the back yard and gave barbecues in it when the weather was warm, and traveled often. When Buck was away he could hear himself walking, all alone in the house; he sometimes thought he heard the big clock ticking in Buck's kitchen downstairs. When he took Buck's letters and newspapers into the vestibule and put them in the growing pile on the mat, he wondered how long the dusty bottles had been accumulating there, and looked through the glass panes in the door to see the bookcase and the coat rack and the painting—of two couples, in boats, on a placid lake— that hung in Buck's hallway.

The woman who lay in the sun in her back yard was as old as he was, possibly older. She lived on the far side of the ground floor of the large house; he had never studied her except from a distance. For a month after he first saw her in her chair he thought she lived on the near side, under Uwe—for a long time he'd wondered who lived in that apartment—but it turned out to be another woman, much younger, with darker skin and hair. Below her were the couple with the toddler. Besides the woman he watched and Uwe, who clipped and pruned, the mother and her little boy were the only ones in the house who used the back yard. He didn't like to think of a family living in a basement apartment, but when he glanced in the windows while cutting Buck's grass one hot spring day it looked very pleasant, comfortable and clean, and the little boy always seemed wildly happy in the yard, racing up the side steps and throwing himself onto his three-wheeler before his mother could catch him, running after the squirrels, waving his arms out of excitement or pleasure or lack of control. The father, he thought, was somewhat stern—a tall thin man with a worried look—but the mother laughed often, and rolled in the grass with her little boy. She spoke with an accent though her husband didn't. When it was dark in his apartment and he looked straight down into their kitchen he could sometimes see her hands, in the bright fluorescent light, moving pans on the stove, breaking eggs, stirring vegetables, taking away the kettle and, seconds later, bringing it back again.

His own home was modest. He had few possessions, a condition that was still very new. At intervals he would wonder where some object was, and even search for it, before he remembered selling it at the yard sale he'd had when leaving the city he'd lived in before, or throwing it away, or leaving it there for his roommates to enjoy. The six of them had shared what had once been the summer home of a wealthy family, a huge house with a vast lawn and spaces they never used, and five ornamental mantels on the ground floor alone. He much preferred living by himself. It was very different; the stream of conversation and casual acquaintance that had washed over and around him in his previous circumstances had so suddenly and thoroughly ceased when he moved that it was as if he'd gone a million miles, not a thousand. He never heard from anyone there, not the roommates he hadn't cared for or the colleagues he'd liked but had never known well, not the women he'd dated and slept with. He was aware of what he'd done to arrange it—the fit of revulsion for everything he owned and his frantic efforts to rid himself of it, the way he'd said good-bye as if barely able to wait, the decision to leave itself, which had been motivated by nothing other than a vague, unsubstantiated notion that he'd overstayed his welcome—but even so the completeness of the change sometimes astounded him. It was as if he'd created something entirely new, with no recognizable source and no beginnings, no first instant. He could stand at the top of the stairs outside his bedroom, the summer evening light coming through the windows and the door and falling on the low bookcase holding the small collection of volumes he'd chosen to keep, and ask, how did I come here?, and not have an answer. He had remade almost everything.

When he watched the woman in the back yard it was private and exciting, an erotic experience, and he wouldn't tell himself otherwise. It was most of what little he had. It wasn't that she was so much uncovered, in her bathing suit or tank top, or that she was vulnerable because she didn't know he was watching; it was something else he didn't clearly understand. He thought it might have to do with him, not with her—his mood, his life, his internal arrangement on the moment he first noticed her there, the first time he looked out through the window and saw her legs against the grass—and that he could make it go away and come back again, as an act of will. There was nothing unusual about the way she behaved. There was nothing particularly special about her—she was fair and of medium height, slimmer and less buxom than the woman on the near side, with a face that seemed perfect on account of the distance and was probably, he knew, just a pretty face—but she was almost irresistibly appealing, painfully so. She made him want to cry.

It was strange, he found, to be so powerfully impelled and so determined to do nothing. He didn't want her, not to sleep with, but he wanted to know her, to examine what she had and share it somehow, while keeping apart. He wanted to sleep with her, but not at the cost it would certainly bring: the loss of what he felt when he watched her in the yard. He thought more than once of touching himself as he stood by the glass, but even that seemed too much of a risk. Once started in that direction he might not be able to stop. She wouldn't know what he was doing, which would break his heart.

When he watched her he thought she reminded him of people from his past, or at least of situations, but it wasn't precise; he'd seen her do the same things with the same simple props so many times that it was hard to tell where she left off and his memory began. Often he had to satisfy himself with a brief impression of something long gone: his sister when they went on picnics, his job with a landscaper in the eleventh grade, the framed poster he'd had in his childhood room, or deep winter nights writing papers in college, staring through the glass over the frozen quadrangle, wondering what he might find and bring back with him to warm him as he worked. If he paid too much attention or gripped too tightly there was nothing at all. She reminded him of Margaret, the first little girl he'd loved, but not, he knew, on account of the physical resemblance; that was a clue, but not the answer. Together she and Margaret resembled something else, something important to him, with a life of its own, a life that had started with his and to which he was still, after all these years, mysteriously bound.

In the hottest days of the summer, as he walked the neighborhood at night, he heard voices coming from the houses and yards. Sometimes they were happy, murmuring, laughing, peaceful, and when they made him feel bad he thought of her, and the only image he allowed himself of the two of them together: she in her lounge chair and he on top of her, sleeping in her arms. There were thousands of people in the area through which he walked, and there was nothing in him or in her that couldn't be found in another nearby. For either or both of them to exist differently—to change the way they lived from day to day, to come or go, to speak—would alter nothing, would not tip any balance, would never add to the range or the depth of what was around them, the lives and times of their immediate world. As he approached his doorway he more than once thought that Uwe's house and his own beside it made an island of independence, or isolation, in the sea of the community; of all the people in them, as far as he could tell, the child and his mother were the only matching fragments, the only ones who were not essentially alone.

One evening, sorting through the mail on the stoop of his entrance on the side of the house, slow to go in because the air smelled so sweet, he looked up to see the dark woman, in pants and brassiere, moving from room to room in dim but revealing light. She was tall and voluptuous. Her blinds had always been closed in the night but now they were open, and he could see her clearly through the slats. His first thought was pleasure at his good fortune; his second, to ask if it was fair to look; his third, that it must be her habit, as it was his, to close the blinds as soon as daylight faded, or when she came home if it was already dark, and that she had some reason for letting it go on this particular evening, for not caring, and that whatever her reason, it had nothing to do with him. She didn't know he was there.

There was a quality so different, so strange, in the way she was revealed to him—the light flowing out to him and finding him there, forcing his attention without his consent—that he was almost shocked, and felt a major pause; it verged on violation, not of her privacy or his self-respect, but of the usual and customary rules. She was lovely beyond what he ever would have guessed. As he watched in the dusk she left his sight, for a less than a minute, and when she came into view again her pants were gone and there were only the two small coverings between him and her nakedness, and in the yellow glow of her lamps she might as well have been naked; it was just the same. For all he knew, if he waited long enough she might lose what little remained and stand before him, at the window, and let him look in her eyes.

He clutched his mail and went inside, turning the lock behind him, counting the steps as he climbed to the top, aware of the weight of his heart. He was sure she hadn't seen him, but when he reached his kitchen and turned off the light and moved silently to the window to look down on her, the blinds were closed and impenetrable; she was gone.

He felt, to his amazement, disappointed and abandoned, the moment not a gift but a permanent burden. He could sense a change and his own deep regret. He knew he would remember, he knew he would want to see her again, and he wondered—say he lived in Buck's house for another million years—if he ever would.

─────────────── · Long Island

THE cars rolled, shining in the sun, from the open mouth of the New London ferry. Terrie and Sandy were in the fourth car from the end, an old dented Volvo. As they went out of the parking lot Sandy turned left and seemed to know what to do; he'd spent his last few minutes on the ferry's deck studying the map, finding their landing point and destination and tracing the roads between. Terrie rolled her window down all the way, enjoying the cool breeze on her sweaty face—Sandy didn't like to turn on the air conditioning— as they followed the other cars through the town.

They stopped at a red light, and Sandy reached down and took a cassette tape from the shelf under the dashboard and put it in the player. They started forward again; he tapped his right hand on the steering wheel along with the music, interrupting himself to shift from first to second and from second to third. "I'd love to get some lemonade or some juice," said Terrie.

"Let's get out of town first," he said. "There must be a store on the outskirts."

They listened to the music for several minutes. She'd been thirsty since the start of the ferry ride but the lines on the boat had been too long at first, and then she'd been distracted—by an argument

146
·

they'd had about an article in the paper—until it was too late to buy anything. As she waited the road became wider and faster, passing through more traffic lights, and they were up to forty-five when Sandy slowed and pulled into the parking lot of a small brick store, set back from the road, between an insurance office and a plowed field with a weathered house at its edge. "I'll sit," he said.

Terrie flinched from the heat and dust and bright sun as she crossed the unpaved lot and went into the store. She walked out again with a plastic bottle of lemonade and a can of cola for him; he started the engine before she'd taken hold of the door handle. When they were up to speed he rolled down his own window, which had been open only two or three inches, and asked, "So what's with this guy?"

"Who? Frank?" asked Terrie.

"Whoever we're going to see now."

"Frank," she said. She sipped from her lemonade. "He's an old friend of my parents," she said. "Very successful. Rich. A friend of my mother's in particular." She looked at him. "I told you all this," she said.

"There are lots of things to remember, Terrie," he said, tapping on the wheel again, his soda resting in a holder by his arm. "I guess I left this one to you."

She shifted to her right, resting her back partly against the door— she checked to see that it was locked—and looked at him.

"Successful at what?" he asked.

"I don't know. Lawyer. Business, maybe."

"You called him from home?"

"Mother did." She moved her head back until it was a little bit out the window, her hair instantly drawn by the wind, waving in the air. Her eyes were closed. Sandy raised the volume of music, very slightly, and they rode for nearly half an hour, she motionless, he tapping quietly on the steering wheel, first with one hand and then with the other.

"I hate this," said Terrie. "I hate freeloading on my parents' friends. Spending our time with total strangers. Just for a free bed and a meal."

"If he's really rich it'll be a lot nicer than a motel," said Sandy.

"Who cares?" said Terrie. "I like motels."

The tape came to its end and started over at the beginning. Sandy switched it off. "This is the first turn," he said, pointing to the sign for a crossing highway. "Another one in ten miles, then straight to his door."

"You could let me navigate sometime," she said.

He laughed. "You'll get your chance," he said. "It's a long trip."

They drove the ten miles to the next intersection, the tape player off, and Sandy turned onto the new route without speaking. What wasn't woods, along the roadside, was fields of growing things, with farmhouses and barns and an occasional fruit and vegetable stand. Terrie wanted to stop and get out, and crouch to examine the green lettuce heads, to see the bugs crawling on them; she wanted to lie down in a cornfield and have Sandy kiss her cheek, and go to sleep.

"Why do we do this?" she asked. "I really dislike it. Just to save a few bucks."

"That's good enough for me," he said. "We don't have very many."

Not long after that he said, "This is his road," and turned left onto a shaded lane, recently blacktopped. For a minute more they were in a tunnel of green; then they emerged into bright sunlight. Looking past Sandy as the road curved to the right, she could see the ocean. She had just a few moments before a hill blocked her view. Soon they were under the trees again.


Frank's house was large, and very attractive; she was a little overwhelmed by the fact that something so expensive could be in such good taste. As he led them into the living room that overlooked the water she searched for things that seemed ostentatious or overdone, keeping a list for her parents. It would be a short list. She would have to tell them the house was beautiful.

Frank appeared to her to be very well and fit for a man of his age, trim and muscular, certain in his movements. He was a little taller than average; his hair was gray but there was a lot of it. His skin looked taut and his light, uneven tan had clearly come from regular outdoor activity. She'd known as soon as she entered the house that he didn't smoke, and she could find no prominent liquor supply; perhaps he kept the scotch in the kitchen cabinet, as her parents did.

"Tell me your name again, please," he said to Sandy. "I'm sorry, but I didn't get it at the door."

"Cameron," said Sandy, offering his hand as he had two minutes before. "But they all call me Sandy."

Frank shook Sandy's hand. He was apparently amused, by the extra handshake or because Sandy hadn't given his last name, or for some reason she couldn't guess. Sandy didn't seem to notice and she was momentarily uncertain, and annoyed with him. She moved closer and took his arm.

"Good friends?" asked Frank, pointing from one to the other, moving only his index finger.

"We hope to be married in two years," she told Frank.

"How wonderful," he said, smiling. "Congratulations."

Again she felt briefly confused. "It's not definite," she said. "We'll be at different schools in Boston next year. We wanted to be near each other, but independent. We hope that will help us decide."

"Our parents want us to go slowly," added Sandy.

"I'm not surprised," said Frank as he gestured at the couch. They sat, and he looked down at them for a moment before taking a chair. "But going slowly isn't giving up. It all comes to the same thing, in the end. As long as you know what you want."

"We want a life together," said Terrie.

"All my friends are jealous of me, on account of Terrie," said Sandy.

"I'm not surprised," Frank said again, looking her over. Though she wanted to be angry she wasn't. As far as she could tell he meant no harm; it seemed almost a formality. This is what happens, she thought, when they choose your friends for you.

"If what I hear is half right you'll have a hard time keeping up with her," said Frank. He grinned at Sandy and then at Terrie, turning quickly away when he saw her expression.

"We consider ourselves pretty well matched," Sandy said, "though that may be conceit on my part."

"If so it's just as well for you to have it," said Frank. He stood. "But you've been driving in the sun. You want something cold to drink. What can I get you? I have soda and lemonade, and at least one beer."

"Anything's fine for me," said Terrie.

"I'd love a beer, but I'd better not," said Sandy. "We still have to find a motel tonight."

"A motel? Don't be ridiculous," replied Frank, sharply and with emphasis. He seemed genuinely offended. "I won't allow it." Turning to Terrie, he said, "From what your mother told me I assumed you'd be staying with me."

"Well, of course we will, if you'll have us," she told him. "We don't want to impose."

"It isn't possible for you to impose," he said. As if that were the last word on the topic—apparently it was, because Sandy sat staring at the coffee table, and she found nothing else to say—he went to the kitchen. "There's beer for everyone," he said.


They sat on the deck, around a wooden table that was too small for the dishes and glasses and silverware on it, and looked across the water at the summer sunset, and down the shoreline as it stretched to the west.

"The only thing that makes this house worth what I paid for it," said Frank. "The view."

"It's beautiful," said Terrie.

Frank turned back to his plate, as if embarrassed, and touched the last of his meal with his fork.

"That was delicious," she told him. "Did you really make it yourself?"

"I did," he said.

"We napped while you worked," said Sandy.

"It's a pleasure. It's my hobby. I do it all the time," He laughed. "But I will admit I was looking forward to impressing you." He looked at Terrie. "What do you kids say? 'Blowing you away,' is that right?"

She shrugged. "That's right," she said. In fact, they hadn't napped; Sandy had put his hands on her and she'd pushed them off, several times, and then they'd had a whispered discussion about it, almost an argument, and Sandy had decided to be hurt and withdrawn. Which was very unfair of him, because he knew she was unlikely to be comfortable enough to have sex in a strange house, not right away. And he must have been aware that Frank could have walked down the hall at any moment, and might have heard. And if this wasn't enough, what Sandy couldn't have known but what she had tried, inarticulately and unsuccessfully, to convey to him was that Frank made her nervous, even frightened, despite her efforts to get beyond it, despite his graciousness and charm, his evident respect and benevolent manner, his desire to please. All those things made her more anxious, not less. It puzzled her. She realized she'd been worried before they ever arrived, about something she couldn't sort out, and she wanted to forget it, to settle it; she resented the amount of attention she'd already devoted to a man she'd hardly met.

She watched him pour wine into Sandy's glass. "More for you?"
he asked her.

"No," she said. "Thank you." She looked into one of the empty
serving dishes. "Do you have any children?" she asked.

"I don't," he said, "and I'm rather sorry about it." He seemed
upset by the question, which surprised her, as he moved his chair
back from the table and turned to Sandy. She saw them hold each
other's eyes for a moment, and pushed her plate slightly away.

"It's a little sad, what happened," her mother had said. "We all
liked Frank more than we liked Dottie, and we never knew the
whole story of what went on between them, but we ended up keeping
her in our circle and excluding him."

"You excluded him?"

"We didn't actually ostracize him, dear," her mother had said,
"but on social occasions it always came down to choosing one or the
other of a broken couple; you couldn't ask them together." She had
been making a salad for dinner. "And the fact is that in those days
you tended to blame the man. Maybe because he was the one you
thought could take it. There was Frank, still with his nice clothes
and his self-confidence and his business friends and his athletic clubs,
and there was Dot, miserable and in tears, with no idea of what to
do. We would have felt heartless if we'd gathered around him and
left her alone in an empty house. And in any case, though we weren't
very fond of her, it wasn't as if she deserved it."

Taking another black olive from the bowl, Terrie had seen her
mother's hand pause, holding the knife, over the tomatoes and the
cutting board. "Did they have any children?"

"Don't pick, Terrie," her mother had said. "Fortunately not."

"Mother," Terrie had asked, "was it Frank's fault?"

Her mother had started chopping again, then stopped and looked
at her, smiling. "You do enjoy blaming men, don't you?" she said.

"It varies," Terrie had said. "Was it his fault?"

Her mother had explained—working through the rest of the

tomatoes, the mushrooms, then the scallions, all in the customary order, taking the dressing flask down from the cabinet and filling it with carefully measured vinegar and oil, adding a little sugar as she always did—that Frank had been known for both his looks and his passions; they had all been puzzled when he married a woman who wasn't very attractive or fascinating or smart. The result was as they'd expected. His ex-wife had never accused him of anything, preserving the last of her own dignity and the greater portion of her friends' sympathies by avoiding any statement of cause. Frank hadn't appeared abashed, or ashamed; he had never defended himself.

"He's been unattached for all these years," her mother had said, "and with the money he's made and the people he knows I imagine he's had plenty of chances to get his fill of whatever he's wanted."

"I'm so glad," Terrie had said, "that I don't have to live in a world like that."

"Like what, dear?"

"Where men think that if they want it and can get it," she'd said, "they're entitled to it." Her mother had looked at her steadily for a moment, then back to the spice rack, choosing between basil and dill.

"At any rate, Mother, I don't think you approve of him."

"But I do," her mother had protested. "I haven't seen him for years, but I like him very much. Haven't you been listening?"

She hadn't known whether her petulance had come from her confusion or the other way around. "I don't know that I want to stay with him, thank you," she'd said.

"Oh Terrie, I think you're overdoing it a bit," her mother had said, walking to the refrigerator, pulling it open. "From what I understand it's an absolutely lovely house, well worth seeing, and in any case he was a good friend—please don't forget that it's your mother who's sending you to him, not some chance acquaintance— and you don't have much money, and it's on your way, and in any case I don't know why on earth there would be any reason for you to refuse." She had by then become almost angry. "This is a very silly line of discussion. I'd like to know how you get me into these things."

Terrie had wondered, off and on, whether she would consider Frank handsome. Now she thought she did. The dark, even hair on his arms and legs interested her—Sandy was almost entirely hairless, and very pale, unlike Frank, and skinny and not very powerful—and she wondered where it ended, or if it continued over his entire body, like the man a friend had once described to her. She liked his haircut, and his shorts and knit shirt were flattering. But of course he looks nice, she thought, he has all the time in the world to devote to it.

"My mother remembers you fondly," she said.

Frank smiled. "I was at your parents' wedding, and they were at mine," he told her, looking at her so that she was unable to look away. "Did you know that?"

"I hadn't realized," she said.

Sandy was watching her with judgment in his eyes. This angered her as always, and she was still upset about his behavior before dinner and had no idea what was bothering him now, but she found she wanted him on her side, rather badly. She turned back to Frank. "Perhaps you'll be at ours," she said.

"That would be a privilege." He put his hands behind his head and looked out at the ocean, at the sky. "I remember sitting in the pew that day and wondering if we would all have children. Wondering what the children would be like." He sighed. "The handsomest woman I ever saw," he said, "and the most deserving."

In bed, naked on account of the warmth, sweating even with the breeze from the fan, they lay apart, a foot of sheet between them.

"I don't really like him," said Terrie.

"What are you talking about? He's a great guy," said Sandy. She shrugged. He reached out and touched her thigh, and she lifted his hand and dropped it on the bed next to him.

"You expected not to like him," Sandy said patiently. "You have no reason other than that."

"Shut up, Cameron, you don't know my reasons," she said.

"What reasons could you have?" he asked, in an even tone. "He's extremely kind to us, insists that we stay here, makes us feel at home. He cooks dinner for us. He tells funny stories, and he's very well read and well informed, but he asks us questions and really listens when we answer. He says such nice things about us. And note he has no objection to our sharing a room. What more could you want?" She said nothing. "How many men his age would do so much to make a couple of high school seniors feel good?"

"People have their purposes," she said.

Sandy snorted as he laughed, a mannerism she had always disliked enormously, and disliked at this moment more than she would have believed possible.

"You're lucky I know you love me," she said, turning her pillow over and smacking it twice with her hand. "I put up with all your teasing and your scorn. But sometimes I wonder why you do it."

"I'm sorry," he said. "I do it because I love you. I keep trying to tell you that." She was turned away from him, but she knew he was leaning over her. "Because I love you so much I can't stand it." She could feel the heat of his breath on her shoulder. "I tease you and joke about other women and act petty and selfish because I love you so much I don't know what to do about it. I have to hide it, or pretend it isn't there."

She counted her breaths, saying nothing. The room was still. They lay quietly together until he switched out the light.

"Terrie, I'm tired. If you're not ready to let me hold your tits now, I'm going to sleep."

"Go to sleep, then," she said. He turned over immediately, and she got out of bed and walked to the window. This side of the house faced away from the water and she could see little. There was a faint halo from the just-rising moon, behind a hill, and the dark mass of the tall trees that grew at the end of the long driveway.

Sandy was already breathing deeply and evenly. She didn't know whether he was actually asleep or just trying to convince her that he wasn't upset, but it helped, to her surprise, to calm her down. She had no idea why she was inclined to think poorly of Frank, and to argue with people about it, and it made her feel slightly desperate; she felt keenly unsure of herself, and wanted to demand an explanation. He's just a man, she thought. A man who once wanted my mother, and wished my father would go on a long trip or leave the room or at least look the other way so he could target her for his lust, for one moment of brutal desire that she would see and recognize and be forced to acknowledge, if only by walking away, so he would know he'd made his mark. That's what he cared about, she said to herself. He never slept with her, never really tried; she couldn't have kept that from me. She wouldn't. At most he embarrassed her, or made her wonder for a minute what it would be like.

She touched the glass, hoping it would be cool, so she could press herself against it and stare at the night. When she saw someone looking at her, through the window, she took her breasts in her hands although she didn't step back, and whimpered momentarily, until she saw it was only the mailbox and a cloud. Sandy didn't move, as she looked over her shoulder, didn't wake at the sound. Still her heart was beating faster.

She badly needed a shower, she knew, and was glad to remember as she slowly came awake that there was a bathroom attached to the room they'd slept in; she could make herself more attractive, at least presentable, before going out to face Sandy and Frank. It was nearly ten o'clock, much later than she usually slept, and Sandy's clothes were gone. She was sure he'd been up for hours. She felt sweaty and dirty and her hair was a tangled mess. Her head hurt. She couldn't seem to clear her eyes, and she was certain her odor was bad; she sniffed at her armpits, then smelled herself all over, and was almost repelled.

The shower was powerful and steady and she enjoyed it for a long time, making it first cool, then hot, then cool again, scrubbing herself thoroughly with scented soap and a washcloth she found hanging on a little hook stuck onto the tiles. As she stepped from the enclosure she realized that Sandy had left the only towel out in the bedroom, on a chair; she had to hop across the bathroom to the closet on the far side to get another, distressed because she was dripping so much water on the floor. Then she thought, who cares?, and tossed the towel onto the toilet, and stood in the middle of the room with her hands on her hips, drying in the air, a growing puddle at her feet, watching herself in the mirror.

She took a T-shirt and her white shorts from her bag, because it was already so hot, and put them on. As she started for the door, she looked down at herself. She searched through her things to find her thin, baggy blue cotton pants, and put those on in place of the shorts, then went out and down the hall to the dining room.

Frank was sitting at the table, drinking coffee and reading the newspaper. He smiled at her as she walked up to him. "Good morning," he said.

"Hello," she said. "Where's Sandy?"

He got up and went to the kitchen, where she saw him take a mug from the counter and fill it with coffee from a glass pot on the stove. He brought it to the table and put it in front of one of the chairs, not next to him but across the table. "If I guess correctly you'll want to start with that," he said, moving a sugar bowl and a small pitcher from his place to hers. "Then you can go and forage for yourself, to see what you want to eat."

"Thank you," she said, taking the seat, extremely embarrassed. She poured milk into her mug and had a sip. Hot as it was, it was very good; she drank as much as she could as quickly as she could without burning her mouth, adding more milk to cool it faster. "Did you have a nice night?" she asked.

"I did," said Frank. "I hope yours was pleasant."

"Very," she said.

"I had an interesting and enjoyable talk with your friend this morning," he told her, holding a section of the newspaper in his left hand and his coffee cup in his right. "I hope you know he has a very high opinion of you."

"I know," she said. She drank more coffee. "I suppose I rely on it more than I should."

"He doesn't think so," said Frank. "If anything, he worries that he hasn't made himself clear. He'd like to do more to show you how much he values you."

She examined her arm; she wanted to reach for a part of the paper, but she knew she could do that only with Sandy, or her parents. "I guess we all feel that way," she said at last.

"I wish I'd been more like him, when I was your age," said Frank. "In fact, I wish I was more like him now. He really touched me." He smiled again, much more distantly than he had since they'd arrived, she thought, and looked briefly at his newspaper. "Sandy walked down to the beach," he told her. "I can give you directions if you want to go looking for him. He said he'd be back soon. It isn't far."

"More coffee first," she said.

"Help yourself," he said. "Excuse me for a minute, I want to finish this story."

She took her cup to the window in the living room and looked out at the view. She couldn't see the beach, just the water. As she drank the last inch of coffee she thought of how different it would be in the house if Dottie and Frank had stayed married. It was hard to imagine a couple or a family living in it; it seemed to be so much of Frank, of one man, and so little of everything else.

He was standing with his newspaper, looking at her. "You're very lovely," he said. "I'd like very much to take you to bed."

"How disgusting, Frank," she said. "How terrible."

"Disgusting?" he asked, spreading his arms wide, looking down at himself. "It can't be that, can it?"

She found her own arms tightly wrapped around her; by trying hard she was able to drop them and let them hang at her sides. She made sure she was standing up straight and took a deep breath, looking him directly in the eye.

He returned her look. "I'm attractive to you, I'd guess," he said. "I know I'm nothing remarkable, and I seem very old, but I can't believe you find me unpleasant. And I can guarantee you everything is in working order. I'm sure your stomach wouldn't turn."

"It's a disgusting way to treat a guest," she said. There was a sharp pain in her belly. "It's a disgusting way to treat the daughter of an old friend, who trusts you."

"What have I actually done?" he asked, hands still spread, as if giving her the chance—it infuriated her—to change her mind and run to his arms. "I've just made a suggestion. I haven't physically approached you."

"What would my mother say, do you think?" she asked. "I suppose she was warning me, in her way."

Frank smiled. "She may well have been," he said.

"I'm much younger than you," she told him, beginning to cry. "You're taking advantage of me. You shouldn't be doing this. Even I know that."

He stepped back and lowered his hands, then put them in his pockets. "Terrie, I apologize," he said. He looked at the floor. "It was an impulse. I wanted you to know how desirable I found you."

"It doesn't gratify me," Terrie said. He stood where he was, and as she looked him over—it seemed a fair exchange—she decided she was interested, even tempted. She knew it didn't matter, because Sandy might come back to the house at any moment, and if he didn't find them at it he would sense it later on. She was enraged by Frank, and thought him contemptible. She would never do it. She wondered what his hairy skin felt like. It was absolutely impossible, so far beyond her that she imagined touching him—he was so much stronger and more substantial than Sandy, so much more like a man—and didn't care that he could see her thinking about it, could follow the ghosts and faint twitches of her impulsive movements. She pictured him holding her, grasping her, and Sandy coming in, seeing the muscular back and the look on her face and knowing at last that she wasn't confined to him, that she could take what she chose. She was helpless between the two of them, the one who assaulted her—he stood there, as if innocent, as if he wanted only her happiness—and the one who counted her as spoils. There was a sound that might have been Sandy, at the door; she saw that her hand was out and her mouth open, and she closed it, and pulled it back.

They stood next to the Volvo in the driveway, under the trees. Frank was entirely at ease; for a moment she thought he would put his arm around her while he chatted with Sandy. They were talking about marine biology and scuba diving. She was very impatient. She was wearing her shorts and a tank top, but even with so little of her covered she was uncomfortable. She knew it would be even hotter in the car, and that the traffic would keep them from driving very fast, but she preferred anything to staying where she was.

"Let's go," she said.

They fell silent, startled. Sandy shrugged and put out his hand. It came naturally this time; when Frank held it and shook it they looked almost the same.

"You've been very kind," said Sandy.

"I wish I could get you to stay longer," Frank said. "Only one night." He looked from one to the other. "I see it's impossible. Well, it's been a pleasure to entertain you." He dropped Sandy's hand and turned to Terrie. "I really mean that. You're fine company."

"We're flattered," said Terrie.

"Thank you very much, Frank," said Sandy, as he took out his keys.

"Yes, thanks," she said. She went to the passenger door and opened it. She looked back at him, and as she swung herself into the seat— she couldn't stop, it would have been too awkward, and she knew she didn't really want to stop, that there was nothing to be done— she saw regret and loss and bitter loneliness on his face, shocking in a man so self-assured and independent, who had led her so easily to the point of abandon, to the illumination of her will. She watched her own hands fastening her seat belt; as Sandy started the engine, she looked in the mirror and found real hopelessness, of a kind she was certain she'd never known, had only had described to her. He was pleading with her. Then he was swallowed up, and washed away.

"Can you believe the nerve of that guy?" asked Sandy, going a bit too fast down the driveway, turning left onto the road without really looking.

"What do you mean?" she asked. "I thought you liked him."

"I did," he said. They went through patches of sun and shade on the narrow road; to their left was the ocean, intermittently visible. "I did until he started asking me all sorts of questions."

"Questions? When?"

"After lunch," said Sandy, stopping at the flashing red light outside the village, turning into the main street, following the signs for the interstate highway. "All sorts of things. Some of them were okay, but some of them were none of his business."

She sat silently and held his hand, but he took it away to work the gearshift as they headed up the ramp onto the highway, where there was no traffic after all. "He was very inquisitive. As if he was never our age." He shook his head. "As if he never went through it himself." He put the car in fifth and settled into the center lane. He turned to her, but she was looking out the window, away from him.

# · To Have,
## To Hold

HE woke up, and understood he'd been dreaming of her. Not in detail, not very precisely, but the worried tone, the laugh, the questions were hers. He realized it in a moment. There were others, and while he was dreaming he thought it concerned them; they were more explicitly represented. But of all the people in the dream, she was the one with no settled place in his life. They were over and done with, or close at hand; she was the one he had reason to dream about, in the way that leads to wakefulness in the quietest part of the night and an uneasy puzzle, to the study of tangled threads that trail away, the ends hard to find.

The last he heard of her was when he missed something—a concert or a play—he'd meant to go to, and was told she'd been there, and was angry at him. He'd known he was the one entitled to be angry; he'd been ready to tell her so. He'd anticipated meeting her and finding the clarity and courage he'd always lacked in her presence. The last he saw of her was on the sidewalk, putting coins in the meter with his half-brother, a much older man, when she walked by, and did not speak but smiled hopefully, and was able to avoid breaking stride when he would not smile in return. His brother, seeing the longing on her face, was intrigued; it was impossible to explain that what she wanted was of no interest to him. He'd since come to understand that what he offered was just as useless to her. It was foolish for either to be angry, or dissatisfied; their association was a matter of chance; they had met for no good reason.

Over time he'd thought of her less often, and less often again. In fantasy, at first, she was always present, though there was so little of fact upon which to build—they had hardly touched, and their intimate moments had been moments of distress—that she was mostly an image with which he could begin before moving on to something that had actually taken place, or might have, or might. Having pictured her body and face there was little to add. As the years passed even that role diminished, and lost its power and its purpose; there were acts they'd committed in his mind, whole scripts he'd written, closely guarded yearnings that had once been important but became minor, insignificant, faded away.

He still cared, for a time, without basis or reason. In her absence his attachment had to justify itself, which it could not do. She became more of an experience and less of a desire and eventually, in a process he was coming to recognize as a part of his life, the passion drained from him entirely and he felt, when he thought of her, a distant relief.

The last he read of her was that she'd married, and now, lying awake in fragile solitude, examining his dreams while he could, comparing the way he'd once thought of her, called to her, ached for her to this strange half-encounter in the dark, he understood that he'd wanted her to be his wife. He was able to say: all this time I had some idea, poorly shaped, of companionship, intimacy, tenderness, protection; it was her. I never asked why I wept; I was not aware of the others around me; I thought I was drawn by some tragic perfume, ruled by a voodoo spell, and all it was, really, was an accident of contact, a trick of vision that allowed me to see in her the possibility of not being alone.

He was grateful for the understanding and felt a satisfaction, as if he'd received new substance on which to draw, or added a cherished object to his collection. He was grateful for the dream because it reminded him that despite their crossing purposes, the pointless stalemate they'd fallen into, she had always cared for him; she had always tried to help. She had actually been very kind. He started to cry, in his disappointment and grief, remembering something she'd said when he called her at an awful time—not a time of crisis, because there was nothing to be done, just the anticipation of unfolding misery—and became very confused about what had followed what: do I remember her this way because I know, now, that she wanted me to be happy, or does that only make it worse? Could I have changed our lives? And where was the failing? In her? In me?

Once, in the middle of the in-between years, he had crossed the river and was waiting for the light to change when a woman ran by; he thought it might be her. It was early in the morning, misty by the water, and he was slow to look again, so he had only the moment to judge by. He knew it could have been her—he was sure this was outside him, not rising from his depths—but it didn't matter, because he could imagine her as if it had. As if they'd never been apart. The picture he made as he drove up the ramp and onto the highway was so pure, so much as she had always been and would always be, that he knew it was essential, and went back to his beginnings; somehow, by some wholly unexplained but entirely natural chance, she lived in him, and had never failed to recall to him the very first things he had looked on with love.